New York Times bes
never imagined tha
a living…though sh
She lives in the Roc
with her husband, tw
two idiot cats. In her non-existent spare time Lauren partakes in far too many hobbies! She loves to hear from her readers through e-mail, Facebook and Instagram! Sign up for Lauren's newsletter here: eepurl.com/OeF7r

If you liked *Playing Dirty*, why not try

One Night Only by JC Harroway
My Royal Sin by Riley Pine
No Strings by Cara Lockwood

Discover more at millsandboon.co.uk

PLAYING DIRTY

LAUREN HAWKEYE

MILLS & BOON

First Published in Great Britain 2018
by Mills & Boon, an imprint of HarperCollins*Publishers*
1 London Bridge Street, London, SE1 9GF

ISBN: 978-0-263-93223-2

MIX
Paper from
responsible sources
FSC® C007454

This book is produced from independently certified FSC™ paper
to ensure responsible forest management.
For more information visit www.harpercollins.co.uk/green.

Printed and bound in Spain
by CPI, Barcelona

For the incomparable Suzanne Rock and Julia Kent,
for not judging me when I said "Little Women" and
"erotic" in the same sentence.

CHAPTER ONE

Then

THIS COULDN'T BE RIGHT.

Ford Lassiter tore his gaze away from the blocky brown house that sat on a large lot shaded by leafy green trees. Looking down at the GPS on his phone, he squinted at the blinking icon that told him he had reached his destination.

"That's just great." He had paid a lot of money for the best that technology had to offer, and now when he really needed his GPS to work? It took him to some run-down estate on the South End instead of the garage he desperately needed to fix his car, which was making a rather ominous rattle.

He was going to miss his meeting outside the city. Nothing to be done about that. Still, he was not accustomed to things not running according to his plan, and it was like an itch that he had no way to scratch.

"Damn it!" Slamming a hand into the center of the steering wheel, he jolted when he accidentally set off his horn. It sent a surge of adrenaline through his system, a shot of caffeine to his blood, and he couldn't help but roll his eyes at himself.

"You can run a small empire without help." Scrubbing his hands over his eyes, Ford took a moment to lean back in his leather seat. "But you can't get your car fixed without an assistant."

The very notion hurt his pride. He had an MBA, for heaven's sake. He was a very intelligent, very rich man.

He could get his own damn car fixed without a babysitter.

Scowling, he once again punched in the name of the garage that the old man at the gas station had recommended—Marchande Motors.

Arrived at destination.

"Okay, then." Either he was going to kill the designer of Google Maps or there was something he wasn't seeing.

He pushed his way out of the low-slung silver Porsche Turbo and took a moment to stretch and look around. He was parked on a quiet street in an old neighborhood, one that looked like it might have been fancy once upon a time but now had clearly seen better days. Unlike the neat grid of downtown Boston, where he spent most of his time, this area was…confusing.

Well-worn family homes were interspersed with the occasional newer model, probably things that had been built after tearing down older ones that just couldn't weather the elements another day. Then there were residences that were little more than shacks. The one that was supposed to house the garage and the one next door to it were stately old estates, though the neighboring house was in far better repair than the one he was currently standing in front of.

Cars were parked on lawns on some of the nicer houses, and pretty flower boxes lined the sills of the poorer places. None of it made sense to Ford. He supposed that it might hold some charm for someone more whimsical than himself, but all he saw was chaos.

He'd had a meeting in a suburb south of the city, and his car had started to make that ominous sound once he'd entered the South End. He'd never actually spent any time here, and, looking around, he could see why.

Pressing his lips together, he rounded the sidewalk of the place he'd been directed to.

"There we go." The old, twisted trees had hidden the fact that the building was on a corner lot. Once he rounded the corner, he could see a driveway and cars lined up in a more or less neat row.

More than seeing that there was more to the house, he could *hear* it—music was blaring, loudly enough that he wondered how it hadn't reached his ears before. He got his answer when he pushed through the verdant greenery and the volume only increased—it had acted as a barrier.

Now that he was through? He winced as the thunderous bass notes threatened to make his eardrums explode.

He recognized the din, just barely, as Metallica, and though he'd so far resisted the urge to look down his nose, this choice pushed him past the point of no return. Who listened to "Enter Sandman" when there were so many more *civilized* options? Like Coldplay.

The plastic sign with crooked letters that identified the garage as the place he'd been looking for did nothing to improve his opinion. It was stuck into the lawn with a wooden stake, and while he thought the words might once have been red, they were now the peachy pink of salmon.

"No way am I leaving my car here." Ford knew he was a bit of a snob, and he was okay with that. He worked hard to live up to the family name—more than his own father had ever done. So what if he enjoyed the perks that came with wealth?

"You dropping off keys or are you going to stand there all day?" a female voice shouted out from the shadowed depths of the garage, jolting him—he hadn't seen anyone inside. Ford squinted into the bright midday sunlight, but he couldn't see the speaker.

He wasn't used to being put on the spot, and he didn't appreciate it.

"It seems I've come to the wrong place." A garage attached to a ramshackle house, music loud enough to deafen him, a woman yelling at him instead of smiling, like he usually encountered—no. Just no.

Spine straight, Ford turned on the heel of his hand-tooled Italian leather shoe and started to walk away.

"If you're looking for another garage, I know for a fact that Jimmy's place is overbooked." *Ov-ah booked.* The speaker's voice had more than a little hint of the Massachusetts accent that he'd tried hard to eradicate from his speech. It should have only served to further annoy him, but he couldn't focus on her voice, not with what she'd just said. "He sent me the job I'm working on right now because he was full up."

Shit. The rattle in his Turbo sounded pretty bad, especially when compared to its usual near-silent purr. Still, he might have risked it...if he could have remembered when he'd last had it serviced.

Turning on his heel, he pulled out his phone and tapped out a text to his assistant, never mind that he'd wanted to prove that he could do this himself. Jeremy replied within a minute, efficient as always.

You're not going to like this, but don't shoot the messenger. It's going to be at least twelve hours until you can get a tow. There's been a huge pileup by the harbor and every truck is there, cleaning up the mess.

Ford ground his teeth together.

What garage are you at? Could you leave the Porsche there and I'll send a car to pick you up?

Down the street a rough engine growled, roaring to life. Ford jolted, nearly dropping his phone.

The engine was followed by coarse language and shouts that had south Boston dripping from their every word.

The Turbo was his baby, the first big purchase he'd made when the money started to roll in. No, he wouldn't be leaving it here overnight.

"Where do I leave my keys?" His voice was tight as he turned yet again and stalked forward. He entered the open door of the garage, scanning the appallingly disorganized shelves and inhaling the heavy scents of motor oil and gasoline.

He still couldn't find the person who'd spoken. *Infuriating.*

"Leave them on the counter there." The voice was coming from below him. Taken aback, he looked down to find a pair of absolutely filthy work boots sticking out from beneath a rusty old Contour—his mystery voice.

"Could you please come out of there so I can speak with you for a moment?" Ford wasn't accustomed to having to ask for things like this, either. When he entered the high-rise in downtown Boston that served as the headquarters for his hotel conglomerate, people snapped to attention. The security guard would smile and wave him through. People held the elevator. On his floor, one assistant would hand him a cup of perfectly brewed black coffee and the other his tablet, the day's schedule already open for him to peruse.

A very unfeminine snort issued from the area of his feet.

"If I come out to talk to you, I'll have to stop working on *this* car. And that will just put the next car behind, and consequently yours." The voice, otherwise sweet in tone, dripped with sarcasm. "And I'm guessing you're the type who's in an all-fired hurry to get out of here, so no, I won't be coming out until I'm done. Leave your keys on the bench, fill out a form, and come back in three hours, or have your car towed back to the north side."

Jeremy had said that towing wasn't an option. This was unacceptable.

"Three *hours*?" Ford was indignant. "That won't work at all. I'll pay extra to have it bumped up the line, but I expect this car to be finished as soon as possible."

His tone was the one he used on the battlefield of the boardroom—the one that always, *always* got him the desired results. Instead?

The feet, which had been tapping in time to the music, stilled. A breath of honeyed vanilla hit his nose seconds before the woman rolled out from beneath the Contour.

He had a brief impression of dark hair and incredibly blue eyes, and then the navy jumpsuit–clad creature was on her feet, not just glaring at him, but actually poking her finger into his chest.

He knew that he wasn't going to win any feminist awards, but he was a bit taken aback that the mechanic was a woman—he'd assumed that the voice belonged to a receptionist or assistant of some sort. Not that he thought women couldn't do any job they wanted—he just hadn't expected it.

"Now just a minute—" He wasn't going to tolerate this kind of treatment from a service provider, not even if she was a woman. No way, no how.

He didn't get a chance to say so.

"*As soon as possible* will be as soon as I finish this car, and the one after that." Those eyes shot out licks of cerulean flames that threatened to incinerate him. "Around here we do what's fair, and what's fair is for you to wait your turn."

"I'm not sure you understand how much money I'm willing to pay—" Ford tried to speak, and the damn woman poked him in the chest again.

"What kind of person bends the rules for money?" She sniffed, tossed back a long dark braid, and Ford again caught that intriguing whiff of vanilla. The scent was so out of place, layered over the engine grease, it made Ford think of cupcakes.

An odd thought for him overall, since he rarely indulged in dessert.

"So you're saying there's nothing I can do to speed this process along?" Ford shook aside thoughts of sweet baked goods and grasped his irritation. He found it especially annoying that he couldn't really see her, this strange creature who had the gall to yell at him—couldn't see the person in the shapeless coveralls or the skin beneath the thick layer of engine grease. She looked like she'd been grubbing around in a coal mine.

The woman gave him a sweet smile, but Ford noted that her eyes—the only part of her that was clearly visible—were still glittering as she did.

"Like I said." She pointed at the desk. "You've already put me behind. So for the love of God, if you want your damn car fixed, go put your keys over on that bench and fill out the form."

"I can't believe I'm stuck here," Ford muttered as he turned to do as the woman said, and he heard a snort of laughter that made him turn back to her.

"Actually, you'll be stuck at the café down the street." Now her expression was mocking. She clearly didn't think much more of him than he did of her. "I don't have a waiting room."

With the smooth movement of someone who had much practice, the strange person lowered herself back down to the rolling thing—what was it called?—and again disappeared beneath the Contour.

Ford's mind quickly sorted through words and phrases, searching for a witty comeback that would put this impudent woman in her place.

He had nothing. Nothing that would convey the deference he was used to receiving to this grease-covered imp who clearly didn't care.

Scowling, he stalked over to the workbench and all but threw his keys down on the unfinished wooden surface. He took up the stubby-nosed pencil and the order form, then shook his head and instead pulled out a business card, which had all of his relevant information. He clipped it to the form.

Marchande Motors
Proprietor, Beth Marchande

So she was not just the mechanic—she owned the whole garage. Ford didn't quite know what to do with that information—the woman didn't fit into any of the preconceived slots he had to classify the female of the species. And he needed to classify—to classify everything.

What was life without order?

It seemed that this strange, vanilla-scented woman would force him to take a taste and find out.

CHAPTER TWO

BETH DIDN'T HURRY the work that needed to be done on the Contour, or on the massive old truck that came after it. When she hurried she made mistakes, and mistakes hurt the reputation of her business.

One customer lost meant money lost, and she and her sisters and Mamesie didn't have a penny to spare. They all hustled to keep them in their family home, and sometimes that meant servicing the cars of assholes when she'd rather tell them to take a hike.

It was late afternoon when she finally scrubbed the grease off her face and arms, then grabbed the keys that the fancy man had tossed onto her workbench—tossed with more than a bit of temper, which made her lips curl up into a grin.

She was laid-back by nature, so her sisters always said, but when someone threatened her notions of right and wrong, she did tend to lose her grip on control. And even the fact that the offender was jaw-droppingly gorgeous didn't ease the weight of his offenses, at least not in her eyes.

"Of course." Lizzie huffed out a breath when she noted the Porsche logo on the key chain. The breath turned to a whistle when she trotted around the corner and saw the sleek silver Turbo parked on the side of the quiet, tree-lined road.

The fancy man was not only sexy...he was *loaded.* She'd just known it—everything about him had screamed north side. What the hell was he doing out here in the South End?

Actually, what was he doing with a ten-year-old Porsche? She was pretty sure he could afford a new one. Still, a Turbo was a Turbo, and she couldn't quite suppress the thrill when she opened the car door. She was halfway in when she realized that while she'd cleaned off her skin, her coveralls were still soaked with grease. And she'd just bet that Mr. Tight Ass would have something to say if she dirtied up his buttery leather seats.

Shucking her dirty coveralls, she rolled them into a ball and tossed them onto the passenger's seat. Clad in the ribbed white tank top and bright pink yoga shorts that she wore beneath, she finally slid behind the wheel.

She couldn't quite hold back the moan as she ran her hands over the steering wheel. Her joy at being behind the wheel of something like this was almost sexual, it felt so damn good.

She grinned as she briefly considered giving herself a handsy little ride on the seat, picturing the man's face if she told him about it after.

Tempting, but not professional. So instead she eased the vehicle forward, wincing as she heard the death rattle.

"Transmission." She didn't have to look—she was a damn good mechanic, and she'd heard that sound before. But she wanted to give the Turbo a full diagnosis, so after pulling it into the garage, she popped the hood, sighing only a little at the whisper-soft swish of the automated lift.

Without bothering to put her coveralls back on, she started to poke at the guts of the beautiful machine.

She was more than a little disgusted with what she saw.

The main problem was, as she'd known, the transmission. The filtration system was clogged, the seals were hardened and the fluid had been neglected. The Turbo was going to need an entirely new part.

Wear and tear was part of owning a car. But this combined with the sludge that passed for oil, the corrosion in the cooling system, the clogged fuel injectors…

She'd bet that the man…what was his name? She grabbed for the form, leaving fresh smudges on the white paper.

Ford Lassiter. Of course. Fancy name for a fancy man. And all those fancy college degrees listed after his name. Anyway, she'd bet that Ford Lassiter had only serviced his car a dozen or so times in the ten years he'd had it, assuming he was the original owner, and she assumed he was.

Irresponsible.

"Is it fixed?"

Beth turned and found the man in question standing in the entrance of her garage, silhouetted by the late-afternoon sun. He was tall, probably a good eight or so inches taller than her own five feet six. His hair was the tawny kind of color that made her think of a lion, and it offset the surprising chocolate brown of his piercing eyes.

He was lean, but his body looked hard, like he did more with it than just hit a gym. The suit he'd been wearing earlier was well cut and clearly expensive and showed off that body quite nicely.

In the hours since she'd sent him away, he'd removed the suit jacket, loosened the tie and unbuttoned the top few buttons of his white shirt. And in sharp contrast to the sleekness of the outfit, he now had an open can of Coke in his hand. Beth highly preferred this look. In fact, as she met his stare and leaned back against the sleek door of the Turbo, she found herself wanting to purr a bit as she took in the view.

Not that he was her type. At all.

"It is most certainly not fixed." Even through her annoyance, she felt a little quiver in her belly when she looked at him—really looked at him. She'd have to have been dead not to.

"What do you mean, it's not fixed?" That handsome face schooled itself into a disapproving frown, and Beth arched an eyebrow.

Sexy or not, he'd best keep some respect in his tone when she broke the news to him.

"When's the last time you had a maintenance check done on this car?" Pushing off from where she lounged, she beckoned for Ford to come look under the hood with her. He hesitated, and she didn't miss the way those dark eyes meandered down her body, which was far more exposed than it had been earlier in the coveralls.

Interesting. Beth had always had a knack for reading people, probably since she preferred to hang back and study them rather than dive right in. That knack was telling her that Ford Lassiter was a man who kept everything in his world under rigid control.

She would have bet money—if she'd had any—that he wasn't that deliberate in checking out a woman unless some part of him wanted the woman to know.

He hadn't moved but was instead regarding her intently.

Well, well, well. The rich man wanted to go slumming, did he? Smirking, Beth crooked her finger again and deliberately swayed her hips as she bent over the open hood.

That leonine power, that tightly coiled control—he would be fun to tease. And, she noted when he finally deigned to saunter over, not bothering at all to bank the combination of curiosity and attraction in his eyes, she couldn't deny that little click that she felt in her gut when their eyes met.

Chemistry. Couldn't make it, couldn't fake it. It was either present with another person or it wasn't… and it seemed that she and Mr. Ford Lassiter had it on the most elemental of levels.

Beside her, he leaned a hip against the Turbo and regarded her with an amused smirk on his own face. Oh, yes, he felt it, too…and unless she missed her guess, he was entertained by the notion of being attracted to a woman like her.

Beth had made it a point to live her life without worrying about what others thought of her, but it still stung when someone, even a stranger, looked at her like she was one of those wild Marchande girls from the wrong side of town. Well, fuck that. She was going to make him want her so badly his head would spin…and then she'd send him packing.

"Can't remember? Even with all those fancy letters after your name?" She tilted her head, looked up at him, waited while he thought back to her question.

"I don't recall." He didn't even have the decency to look ashamed about it, though she noted that his spine stiffened a bit in defense. "I'm a busy man."

"Seems to me that a busy man like you would

have people who could take care of little details like car maintenance for him." Though Beth's lips curved in a smile, inside she went from irritation to anger. "This fancy machine here? Most people in this neighborhood have to work for five years to earn that kind of money."

She wouldn't focus on what she and her sisters could do—could pay off—with that kind of cash. Replace the furnace that threatened to quit every winter. Patch the place in the roof that let the rain in. "Some of those people might think that you'd want to take care of something like that. Take some responsibility."

"You're right." There, finally, was evidence that he was human—the tiniest flicker of guilt. It was enough to melt her anger away.

Likely he hadn't ever thought about how long other people would have to work to pay for one of his toys...and why would he treat it as anything special when he probably had a garage full of others at home?

"Can I get that in writing? I think it's probably not something you say very often." Beth arched an eyebrow. Ford blinked at her, seemingly stunned, before bursting into laughter.

It was a rich laugh, not the carefully controlled chuckle she would have expected from him, and it cut her off at the knees. To her, nothing was sexier than a man who could laugh at himself.

"Don't get used to it. It probably won't happen again." As if he realized that he'd let his control slip, Ford's grin quickly morphed back into stern lines. "In all seriousness. Now that we've established I don't take proper care of it, what is wrong with it? Do you not have a part that I need?"

Beth couldn't hold back the snort of sarcasm that slipped from her throat. "Well, that's a start, but no, I don't typically carry parts for cars like these. Not much call for them around here."

Doing her best not to roll her eyes—they were clearly from such different worlds—she rubbed her hand over her cheek. The return of his smirk told her she'd likely left a smear of engine grease behind on her clean skin, but she didn't care. That was her. Take it or leave it.

"Your transmission is shot. That needs to be replaced. I can call in a favor and have the part couriered in for the morning, since I figure you're probably willing to pay the rush fee. But replacing it is going to be a full-day job." She held up her hand as he opened his mouth, looking like he was prepared to argue. To her way of thinking, there was nothing to argue about here. "But if you stay consistent with the way you treat this car, then I would suggest you let me fix everything else that's wrong with it while you've already got it in the shop. Your fuel and cooling systems need work, you've got some corrosion… and you need a basic damn oil change."

"I see." Ford gazed at her steadily, his expression unwavering. Beth stared right back, startled when he was the one to break away, huffing out a sound of exasperation and waving his hands in the air. "*What* are you listening to?"

"Sitar music." She loved this playlist as much as she'd loved the heavy metal one she'd been playing earlier. Music was so deeply ingrained in who she was, she felt it was a shame not to appreciate as much of it as she could.

"Right." This, finally, this was what seemed to throw him off his game—the music blasting from her phone.

Beth felt her breath catching as he reached out and sifted his fingers through the end of her braid. Her breasts pushed forward as she exhaled, and Ford looked her over again with that hungry stare—not lecherous, just an acknowledgment of that strange little click between them.

Beth didn't believe in love at first sight…but oh, she sure believed in lust.

"Sitar music. Heavy metal. Purple in your hair, and the scents of vanilla and engine grease on your skin." He sounded bemused. "Has anyone ever told you you're a very unique woman?"

"All the time." She was pretty sure it was a bad idea, but the way this strange man was looking at her made her very, very hot. Riding on instinct, she reached for the cherry-red can of Coke that still dangled from his fingers and lifted it to her lips. "But you've only scratched the surface. There's a lot more to me than the color of my hair."

"I can imagine." He watched her with painstaking attention to detail as she lifted the can to her lips and sipped. The rush of sugar burst over her tongue, and she imagined she got just the slightest taste of him, as well.

"Are you always this forward?" He tracked her tongue as she ran it over her lips.

"Afraid of catching girl cooties?" Beth handed the can back and arched an eyebrow. "And yes, I often am. I'm usually pretty clear on what I want."

Stepping away from where they were still curled together beneath the hood of the Turbo, she laced her hands together and dipped her head. "But sometimes I like to be told what to do, too."

Her heart pounded as she made the admission. Had she judged wrong? She couldn't have. She liked to go after what she wanted, true enough, and she felt no shame in wanting what she did. But she usually felt the subtle little click that she had with Ford when the dynamics between them were just right—as in, the other person wanted to be in control, and Beth wanted to relinquish it.

"I..." Ford took a step back, not the reaction that Beth was expecting. He looked her over again, and her skin felt on fire everywhere his gaze touched.

No, she wasn't wrong. She felt it in her gut. But he didn't seem to be all that pleased by the notion.

"I'll tell you what to do, then." The struggle to regain control was evident in his voice. One blink of her eyes, and the stern businessman mask was back in place, shuttering the hint of passion that she'd glimpsed below. "Order the part. Fix the car. And call me when it's ready for pickup."

Beth felt the same slight chill that she had when she'd noted that he seemed uncomfortable with whatever this was sparking between them—felt it and resented it.

She wasn't asking for a ring—she was just embracing her needs and desires, like she and her sisters had always done.

"You didn't ask how much the parts and work are going to be." Beth's temper rose, so she unlatched and slammed the hood of the Turbo closed, hard enough that most people would have turned to check that she hadn't taken a golf club to the metal.

He didn't turn, didn't look back—not at the vehicle and not at her.

"Like you've pointed out already… I can afford it."

Well, then. Clearly he wanted to highlight the differences between them. Beth cocked her head and watched as he headed out of her driveway and back in the direction of the café, probably off to research his accommodation options, which she could have told him were few. She suspected he wasn't going far.

His gait was easy, the stride of a man who knew that he had the world at his feet. As if pulled by her gaze, he finally cast one look back in her direction.

The intensity of the connection when their eyes met nearly brought Beth to her knees. Yes, that attraction was there, burning brighter than any she'd ever felt.

So why was he turning away from it? From her?

She could dwell on it, could go cry into a bottle of wine with her sisters over the rejection, but she'd never seen the point. Sex was supposed to be easy, fun. And to her it always would be.

If Ford Lassiter was uncomfortable with being attracted to her, well, that was his problem. Beth was just fine with who she was. Still, it was a damn shame he was a stick-in-the-mud, she thought as her lips curved.

A man who looked that good *in* clothes? He would surely look even better out of them.

CHAPTER THREE

THE SURFACE OF the bar was sticky beneath his hand as Ford placed his whiskey glass back down. It was his second of the night, and he felt like he needed to indulge in at least one more, just to get his head back on straight.

He'd been feeling off center ever since the interlude with a certain little mechanic that afternoon. Damned if he could entirely understand why.

"One more?" Even in the dingy bar that was connected to the equally dingy motel he'd had no choice but to book a room in, the bartender who approached him was still more his type than the woman who'd laid into him about responsibility that afternoon. Tall and slender, with icy-blond hair and a neat sleeveless blouse, she more closely resembled the women he dated back in the city.

Neat. Proper. Nice.

He considered for a moment, contemplated indulging some of this frustration in a flirtation with the blonde. Maybe it would lead to a nice dinner and some equally nice sex.

Before he could consciously decide, his hand covered his glass. "Not right now, thanks."

There was a flicker of disappointment in the blonde's eyes as she nodded and walked away, and Ford cursed himself. *That* was the kind of woman he should be attracted to.

Curvy mechanics with rainbow-bright ink snaking over their pale skin didn't belong in his life. Not even for a night. And not because of that brightness…but for other, darker reasons.

Settling back on the stool where he'd been seated since the need to escape the shabby motel room had clawed at his skin, Ford blocked out the thunderous music from the old-timey jukebox and allowed his mind to pull up the image of her—of Beth Marchande.

Nothing about her made sense.

She moved like she couldn't care less about anything but was quick to speak up when she had something to say. Confident—she was quietly confident, owning her curves in a way that stick-thin women he knew back home didn't seem capable of.

Her hair, in that long, thick braid, was midnight black up top and twisted with bright purple below. *Purple…*what kind of woman had purple hair?

And yet he couldn't stop imagining it wrapped around his fist as he thrust into her.

Jesus. He needed to get a grip or he'd embarrass himself in the middle of this dive bar.

He'd been in her presence for less than an hour, and yet he already knew he'd never forget her. She was too vibrant to ever be erased.

"Forget about it." He'd fucked it up that afternoon by being an asshole, he knew that. It would be best to signal that sweet blonde bartender and order another drink, to forget all about Beth Marchande of Marchande Motors.

But damn it…when she'd stood there, hands clasped submissively in front of her? When she'd issued that invitation, had said she liked being told what to do, while he could just make out the outline of a barbell piercing her right nipple, pressed against the tissue-thin fabric of that skimpy shirt?

She'd pierced right through to the core of his basest desires, the ones that he tried with an iron fist to keep locked away and buried.

Lots of men with his power, his position, indulged in all sorts of hedonistic things, and he didn't judge them for that. But after seeing his father go through wife after girlfriend after mistress, treating them all like his possessions?

As far as Ford was concerned, nice men didn't have the urge to tie their women up. Didn't have their palms tingle with the need to redden white skin, to leave a mark of mastery.

The tattooed little mechanic made every one of

those latent desires come roaring to the surface, threatening to boil over.

That just wouldn't do.

And yet here he was. He hadn't been willing to be far away from the Turbo, sure, but that wasn't the only reason that, instead of calling a car to take him home, he'd taken a room in the one small motel he'd been able to find close to the shop.

The woman had hooked him. He was interested, even if he didn't want to be.

Bad idea, Ford. Very bad idea.

"Excuse me?" Lifting his head, Ford raised his hand to signal for the bartender again. He'd have that third drink, and then he'd go take a long, cold shower. He'd work from his motel room until his car was ready, and then he'd go, as fast and as far as he could.

Out of reach of temptation.

The volume of the music increased with the next song, something slow and sultry that he didn't recognize. Down the length of the vinyl-covered bar, a large young man wearing work boots stumbled onto a stool and slapped a fiver down. "I need a beer, Sallie, and I need it now. There's one hell of a show goin' on over there, and I'm thirsty."

"Coming right up, Ned." Ford watched as Sallie—the cool blonde—slid a longneck across the bar to the rough-looking man. The bartender then leaned against the length of covered wood, looking off in the direction the man had come from, and the man looked that way, too. Both seemed to be settling in to watch a show.

Ford followed their gaze, and lust was an instant, heated punch to the gut.

His sexy little mechanic was on the dance floor, and she was working it.

Torn, faded jean shorts cut off high on her shapely thighs, barely covering an ass that was curved enough for a man to get a good grip on it. A white lace camisole on top revealed enticing flashes of skin as well as a black bra that held her full breasts up nice and high.

Black leather boots with high spiked heels wrapped the length of her calves and all the way over her knees. He could imagine her with nothing but those boots on, hands clinging to his headboard as he moved, hard and fast, between sweetly spread thighs.

She was gorgeous. Not his type at all, with the crazy hair and the tattoos spilling over her collarbone and arms. But on her, it worked. He shifted uncomfortably and noted that it seemed to work just fine for him, too.

"Damn." Ford couldn't hold back the groan as Beth shifted, stepping into the light, and he realized that she wasn't alone. No, she had a woman at her front, a man pressed to her back and her eyes closed, her expression dreamy as she rocked between the two bodies, every movement sensual and sure.

The man behind her was dark and swarthy, and Ford might have thought to be jealous if he hadn't been so fascinated with the way the man fisted Beth's hair and pulled her head back. What he'd seen of her today said that she'd protest being forced to do anything, but her lips, shiny with red gloss, opened with a moan that he couldn't hear but that resounded in his head regardless.

The woman in front of her, a redhead in a tight dress, rubbed her breasts against Beth's own. Ford shifted on his stool, his cock hardening fully as the woman dipped her head and licked a slow trail down Beth's neck.

Damn.

As if he'd spoken out loud, Beth's eyes fluttered open. Lifting her head, she looked across the bar, over to where he sat, aching…and right into his eyes.

Earlier today her eyes had been the color of the afternoon sky, but now they were sapphire fire, the flames licking along his skin. His gut tightened as she smiled lazily, then slowly, sensually disengaged herself from the tangle of limbs.

Behind her, the couple continued their dance, but Ford didn't care—his eyes were on the woman who was crossing the room toward him with slow, deliberate undulations of her hips.

"Fancy meeting you here, Sir Lassiter." She

stopped well into his personal space, and that vanilla perfume made his mouth water and his jaw clench.

"*Sir?*" He arched an eyebrow and tried really hard not to do what he wanted, which was to reach out and place his hands at her waist, to slide her shirt up and feel the warmth of her skin beneath.

"Mmm, you seem like a *sir*." Beth smiled and inched closer, stepping right between his spread thighs. He felt his expression darken—she knew exactly what she was doing, what she was asking for.

"What makes you say that?" His instincts told him to tug her flush against his body, to press her to him so she could feel exactly what she was doing to him.

He did not.

"You seem all proper and noble...like an aristocrat. A knight. Sir Lassiter." Beth nudged forward just a whisper, and he felt the curve of her hip press into his inner thigh.

His mouth went dry.

"Like you're trying so hard to do what you think is right. But tell me something." Tilting her head back, she looked up into his eyes, searching. "Why is denying yourself something that you want, that we both want, the right thing? I know you feel it, too."

Her open question gutted him. He'd been in the boardroom with billionaires, with sheikhs, with sharks, and he'd bested them all.

The little woman who smelled like cupcakes? She was bringing him to his knees.

"I—" He started to explain, but she cut him off, stepping back, her sudden frown breaking the spell.

"I see." Her lips pinched together in a mockery of a smile. "I'm not the kind of woman you want to get involved with, right? Not even for a night. Let me assure you, that's your loss."

Wait…*what*?

"Wait just a damn minute." When Beth would have turned, Ford did as he'd imagined, catching her by the waist and hauling her back into the vee of his legs. This time her pelvis connected with the steel length of his erection, and he savored her sharp little intake of breath. "What do you mean?"

"I think it's pretty self-explanatory." Beth regarded him coldly, though she didn't back down. "My hair, my tattoos… I'm far too wild for you."

"Oh, do you think so?" The way she was looking up at him, so certain she was right, was a challenge, and he felt something inside him roaring to life to meet it.

She thought he was turned off because she wasn't his usual type? Well, he couldn't deny that she was not at all the kind of woman he was usually drawn to, and his instant attraction to her puzzled him more than a bit.

But that wasn't the problem. The problem was what she made him *feel*.

"I don't give a damn about the color of your hair or the ink on your skin. Got it?" The need to prove that she wasn't the problem was quickly overriding his sense of restraint, the only other thing that had held him back from accepting her sweet offer that afternoon.

"I don't know you, yet you make me want things I'm not comfortable wanting. Make me feel things I shouldn't." His hands at her waist squeezed, hard, to emphasize his point, and he savored her resultant shudder, which ratcheted up his own excitement.

"Why would you be uncomfortable wanting something if it doesn't hurt anyone else?" She was watching him again, lids heavy over those big eyes. "Or maybe you think that it *is* hurting someone?"

He kept his stare on her face, absorbing every nuance of her expression, which was open, honest.

Something told him that Beth Marchande wasn't going to be disgusted with the demands he might make of her.

"Sometimes a little bit of hurt is good, Sir Lassiter...especially when I'm begging you for it."

"Fuck." Dragging his hands up her sides, over her rib cage and the swell of her breasts, Ford clasped Beth by the shoulders and tugged her forward, crushing her smirking lips to his own.

Rather than offering him a kiss as sweet as the vanilla she smelled of, she moaned beneath the pressure and opened, her tongue surging out to tangle with his.

One hand slid behind her head and fisted in the

long mane of raven and amethyst hair, just as his fingers had itched to. He tugged her head to the side roughly and then dragged his lips down the column of her throat, settling over her pulse and sinking his teeth in to claim.

"Well, what's it going to be, Sir Lassiter?" Beth's breathy question rasped in his ear, and she shuddered when his teeth marked her skin. "Are you going to be good? Or are you going to be bad? What do you think?"

Shoving his glass aside—he felt intoxicated just from being near her—Ford stood, making sure that every plane of his body glided against hers as he did.

Her eyes glittered with the same need that he felt as he quickly pulled a fifty from his wallet and tossed it onto the surface of the bar.

"I think..." Ford deliberately wrapped his fingers around her own, drawing them up to his lips to nip. "I think that we're going to go back to my room right now. And I'm going to find something better for that smart mouth to do."

CHAPTER FOUR

WHAT AM I DOING?

This woman was different. Exotic. Wild. Not like anyone he'd ever been drawn to before, and he wasn't sure why he was attracted to her now. He didn't do exotic, didn't want wild.

And yet when he placed a hand at the small of her back to guide her out of the heated bar, he swore he almost felt a physical shock from just the press of his fingers to that small dip in her spine.

The Turbo had been his first acquisition on the road to success. He'd kept it because nothing had ever felt as good as that first achievement. That first marker of success that he'd earned on his own, not riding on his parents' coattails.

Over the decade since its purchase, he'd bought and sold cars, property, investments. Had pursued some of the most interesting and beautiful women in the world. Had grown his small hotel chain into something internationally renowned.

Nothing had come even close to recapturing that

thrill, the high of knowing he'd achieved something on his own.

Nothing, that was, until now.

Beth said something to the giant man standing by the door as they passed, making the other man laugh. Then they were outside, the cool air of early fall in Massachusetts as refreshing as a swim on a hot day after the beer-soaked heat inside the bar.

He watched as she shook her long fall of wavy hair back. The bright purple seeming ethereal and mysterious in the fading light.

What was going on with him? Purple hair wasn't sexy. Full-sleeve tattoos weren't sexy.

Except that on her, it was.

He stuffed his hands into his pockets as she looked him over. Those blue eyes of hers seemed almost to glow, full of wicked intent as she took her time regarding him from head to toe.

His body responded, dark need curling tightly in his gut. No, he had no idea why he wanted this woman so badly, but he did, wanted her with a craving that seemed primal in its intensity.

"I'd invite you back to my place, but I could tell this morning it wasn't exactly your cup of tea." She smirked at him, a knowing little smile that made his mouth water. She was provoking him deliberately.

That exchange they'd had earlier in the garage. The dynamic between them. Unless he'd read it very,

very wrong, she wanted the very thing that he tried hard not to offer.

"Clearly you didn't think I was serious about finding something better for your smart mouth to do." He couldn't help it. The needs that he was usually fine ignoring were clawing beneath his skin, begging to tear their way free to be with her.

The sharp inhalation of her breath was confirmation. An ache spread through his core.

Nice men don't want this.

Then maybe he wasn't a nice man.

"Coming?" Arching an eyebrow at him, Beth turned and started to walk in the direction of the motel. He couldn't have stopped himself from following.

The small rectangle of parking lot was bordered on three sides with rooms. He'd been assigned to room twelve, and when he'd checked in earlier he'd been unimpressed by the cheap floral bedspread, the rough green carpet and the dated lighting, though at least the place was clean. Now he noticed nothing but Beth as she kicked the door closed behind them, seating herself on the edge of the bed and looking up at him with a hint of mockery in those insanely blue eyes.

He wanted to fist his hands in the long waves of her hair and taste her lips again, to touch her until she was breathless and all traces of that mockery were gone. He wanted to flip her over and bury himself inside her.

He needed to get a grip, needed to take the control back. So far she'd hinted at what she wanted but had been the one in the driver's seat.

No more.

"Do you like wine?" The hinges on the small minifridge whined as he opened it. Earlier he'd refrigerated a bottle of the best chardonnay he could find at the tiny grocery store on the corner. He was stymied when he realized that he didn't have a corkscrew.

Frustration mounted. He was supposed to be in charge here. Why couldn't he grab hold of it?

"Need this?" Not bothering to hide her grin at his discomfort, Beth opened the bedside drawer. There, next to a worn copy of the Bible, was a waiter's corkscrew.

"Spend much time here?" He held back a growl of frustration as he took the offered tool, expertly pulling the cork from the bottle of wine. There were so many feelings, so many sensations pressing on his chest from the inside out that he couldn't even raise an eyebrow at the fact that he was pouring the pricey wine into water glasses.

"I've been here before, yes." Beth took the glass from his hand. Lifting it to her nose, she inhaled, then looked up at him. "And probably for exactly the reason you're thinking. Does that bother you?"

Did it bother him? The idea of her with other men?

He wanted her, but he didn't know her. He shouldn't care what she'd done before.

He didn't care for the thought of other men touching her when his own cock was aching to be between her soft thighs.

"Drink your wine." Deliberately, he refrained from answering her question. Crossing in front of her, he watched as she took a sip, puzzled by the expression that crossed her lips after she'd sipped. "What is it?"

"I'm more of a beer girl." Lips twitching, she set the glass aside. Then she crawled to her knees on the bed, making herself right at home. Rising so that she was almost at eye level with him, she looped her arms around his neck and ran her tongue over her lips. "But I'm not here for a drink."

"What are you here for, then?" Reaching behind his head, he caught her hands in his own, holding her there. He countered her direct stare with one of his own, triumph surging when she broke, looking away first.

"Well, Sir Lassiter." Licking her lips again, she tried to pull back, her breath catching when he held tight, keeping her in place, her breasts almost brushing across his chest. "I think we've established that there's chemistry here. I'm here to see what you want to do about it."

His control snapped, the last whisper of wariness

evaporating in a sizzle of flame. *Sir.* That mocking mouth, calling him *sir.*

He didn't want to analyze why he wanted her or why he shouldn't. He didn't want to hold back.

"I—" Still, the words stuck in his throat, even as his hands slid along her upper arms, over her back, tracing a line down her spine.

"I think you told me you had something for my smart mouth to do." Arching into his touch like a kitten in the sun, she fisted her hands in the hem of her top, lifting it up and over her head. He broke his hold long enough for her to toss it to the ground, then groaned when he saw what had been hiding beneath.

Her breasts were perfect. A little more than a handful, soft globes that sat high on her slender torso. The bra she wore was black lace, a pattern that let him clearly see the outline of full pink nipples beneath. One was pierced through with a small silver bar, and the sight of that naughty bit of jewelry, rubbing against the lace, was sexy as hell.

He wanted to place his cock between those sweet curves and let go.

Real men didn't do that.

She noticed his hesitation. Making a sound somewhere between a hum and a sigh, she cupped his cheeks in her hands, forcing him to look right at her.

Like he could look anywhere else.

"Look." Her eyes searched his face, and there wasn't even a hint of hesitation in the blue depths.

"I'm here because I'm pretty sure that we want the same thing—a night of incredibly hot sex. *Dirty* sex. Why don't you stop thinking so hard and just let go?"

God, she was demanding. He didn't usually like that, either, but at her words, something inside him surged to life—all of the wants that he usually kept buried down deep.

She had made it clear that this was what she wanted. What would the harm be in letting himself revel in it for just one night?

"This mouth of yours." Dipping his head again, he brushed his lips over hers, taking the kiss deep fast. His tongue probed at the seam of her lips, and she opened for him, humming with approval as he stroked it over hers. "I think I had something for it to do."

"I think you did," she agreed, planting her hands on his pec muscles. She squeezed a tiny bit, scoring him lightly with her nails as her hands traveled down. Stroking over his stomach, she hooked her fingers in the waist of his suit pants.

"Mmm." Her touch brushed over the head of his cock, which was fully erect and caught in the waistband of his boxer briefs. "Yes, I think we very much want the same thing. Unless you're this happy about something else."

"I'll be happier when you do what you're told." Had he really just said that? He'd been raised in Boston society. The women he usually dated would be horrified. He might have even gotten slapped.

Beth just grinned.

His stomach muscles quivered when she undid the button at his waistband, then slid the zipper down. The metallic rasp grated at air that was suddenly thick with tension. With need.

He tugged at his pants, pulling them down around his hips. His cock sprang free, and, going on instinct, he took his shaft in his fist.

"That's a good look for you, Sir Lassiter." Pushing him away from the bed with a gentle shove on his hips, she slid to the floor. Rising to her knees, she rested her palms on the tops of his thighs. "I bet this is a good one for me."

Lust centered in his groin, a physical ache. When was the last time he'd had a woman on her knees for the sole purpose of sucking his cock? High school, probably. He enjoyed getting head, but he never demanded that a woman get on her knees for him. It was one of those things he wanted so badly that he didn't dare let himself ask. That he assumed a woman did only because she wanted to please, not because she got anything out of it.

Looking down at Beth on her knees, her lips wet and ready, he knew that she was getting just as much out of this as he was.

Their stares locked as he slid a hand into her hair.

Massaging her scalp, he guided her head forward until her lips brushed the head of his cock.

They both shuddered. Before he could take a breath, her fingers joined his, wrapping around the length of his shaft.

Her mouth closed around him, a hot, wet embrace. She sucked him in, and his eyes nearly rolled back in his head.

He never let himself play like this, edging onto something shadowy that both tempted and terrified him.

But it felt so damn good.

"You're good at that." His voice was raw. She looked up at him, and though he couldn't see a smirk on her lips, it was there in her eyes. He couldn't help but grin in return. "Of course, sassy as you are, I'm probably not the first to want to keep it occupied."

As if he'd challenged her, she slid her hand down his shaft, nudging his fingers out of the way. She worked him up and down with a tight grip as she took him deeper into the silky heaven that was her mouth.

His free hand joined the one fisted in her hair, and soon he was helping to guide her movements as she worked his shaft. Pleasure started to build at the base of his spine, and his hips started to thrust.

He needed to stop her before he came in her mouth. Needed to see to her pleasure first. He wanted to make her come before he took her, wanted her weak and wrecked because of what he did to her.

He wasn't at all expecting her to cup his balls in one hand and tug gently. Her nails scored a light path over the tender seam, something no one had ever done to him before, and he saw stars.

"Beth. Beth!" He tried to pull her head back. She hummed around him, the vibration working through his cock, and scraped those nails gently over his seam again. "Oh, fuck."

His release shot from his very core. He pulsed into her mouth, and rather than being repelled, she wrapped her lips around him tightly and swallowed him down. He watched the lines of her throat, transfixed.

Who the hell was this unearthly creature? And where had she been hiding his whole life?

She continued to lick him as he softened against her tongue, finally letting him slide from her mouth. The air of the room was cool after her heat.

Panting, he took a moment to simply look down at her, searching her features for some hint of discomfort.

Instead she grinned up at him, then climbed back up onto the bed. Crawling across it on her hands and knees, she sat back on her heels and looked over her shoulder at him as she undid her bra and tossed it aside.

"My turn."

CHAPTER FIVE

Why wouldn't he just let go?

The man was a caged beast, his dominance rattling the bars. Beth couldn't understand why, after all the reassurances she'd given him, he seemed to think he still needed to hold back.

She huffed out a breath of surprise when he caught the bra she'd just tossed aside.

"Nice reflexes." She smirked at him, wondering if she was going to have to keep hold of that dark edge of his all night to keep it from sliding back beneath the surface. She exhaled sharply when he lifted the scrap of black lace and let it dangle.

"I like this." He tossed it to the floor, then with a move she didn't see coming, pulled at her feet, making her tumble to the bed. He rolled her so that she was lying across the bed face up, and then he was straddling her hips.

His cock still hung free, swollen, red and damp from her mouth. Her stare moved between it and the way he was undoing the front of his shirt, each button revealing another inch of rock-solid torso.

He'd been hiding one hell of a body beneath that suit. Whatever he did for work that required that suit, he countered it with some serious sweat at the gym.

She wasn't about to complain.

His expression was so intense as he looked down at her that she almost—almost—felt the urge to cover her naked breasts. The piercing through her right nipple. She didn't, though, instead waiting to see what he would do. If she would have to prod him, or if he would let go.

"Do the bottoms match the top?" With a wicked grin, he worked a hand underneath her, sliding up along the back of her thigh to cup her ass beneath the abbreviated hem of her cutoffs. He squeezed, and she pressed into the sensation of her bare skin in his palm.

"Doesn't seem to be much of them, whether they match or not." He moved his hand around to the front of her hip, then to the crease where her thigh met her torso. He grazed the silky fabric of the thong she'd changed into along with this outfit, and she let out a shaky moan.

"Lift." The cutoffs slid down easily when he tugged. Leaving them at midthigh, he sat back on his heels and took his time looking her over.

"They do match." He arched an eyebrow, and she felt flushed everywhere his stare traveled—her breasts, her belly, her hips, her thighs. Her center. "I didn't think they would."

"You make it sound like a bad thing." She wanted to part her thighs, to feel his weight between them, but with the shorts still halfway down her legs, she couldn't. "You seem like the type to send full sets of matching lingerie to your girlfriends. Garters, stockings and all."

"Oh, it's a horrible thing," he agreed. With steady movements, he tugged the shorts the rest of the way down her legs. Propping herself up on her elbows, she reached for the zipper on one of her boots, but he stopped her with a raised eyebrow.

"The boots stay on." He worked the shorts down over the leather that stretched all the way up over each knee. "But those matching panties have to go."

"Obviously," she agreed, her voice breathy as he tugged the scrap of fabric down to her ankles, then helped her free each foot. Letting the thong fall to the floor, he surprised her by tugging her across the bedspread until her ass was flush with the edge of the bed.

Oh, yes. Her thighs quivered at what was to come. This was going to be good.

Some men didn't like dropping to their knees for a woman, but Ford did so as he did everything—with confidence. Hell, even when she damn well knew that he was holding back from really delving into that streak of dominance that kept slipping out of him, he still carried himself with ease. A man who was sure of his place in the world.

Beth was comfortable with herself, but her place in the world still hadn't been defined. His confidence drew her like a bee to pollen.

Arching her back, she tilted her head, enjoying the sensation of her hair against the heated skin of her back before letting herself fall back to the mattress. When he closed his large hands around the insides of her thighs, she sucked in a breath and shut her eyes.

"You keep those eyes open." He squeezed, the pads of his fingers digging into her skin. She did as he said, looking down the length of her naked body to where he knelt. He'd tugged his pants back up around his hips but left them undone. She could see the head of his cock, which was on its way to hard again, sliding out the slit of his boxer briefs.

His taste was still on her tongue, and yet her mouth watered. She wanted everything he had to offer.

"Eyes open," he reminded her sharply when her eyelids started to flutter again. "I want those eyes on me. Want you looking at me when you come, fully aware of just who it is that's making you feel so good."

"I'm not likely to forget." She let out a shaky laugh that quickly turned into a moan when he slapped that same soft skin.

She thought he would talk more, would continue

with those dirty little words that seemed so strange coming from a man like him and yet suited him perfectly. Instead he pushed her thighs open wider, catching one ankle and arranging one of her legs over his shoulder.

She quivered as she waited for that first touch of his tongue, his breath fanning hot and damp over her folds. She caught his gaze as he lowered his head, and the intensity in those stormy eyes took her breath away.

He could deny it all he wanted, but the bossiness suited him. Dominance suited him. And if he'd just grab hold of it with both hands, he could blow both of their minds.

His mouth descended. He pressed a hot, open-mouthed kiss to the cleft between her legs, and she shifted her hips beneath him. Nuzzling his nose between her folds, he licked her from top to bottom, then bottom to top, and a soft cry escaped her lips.

"You're wet. Soaking." He swirled that tongue around her clit. "You liked sucking my cock, didn't you?"

She moaned, then cried out when he delivered a light slap to her inner thigh again. "Answer me."

"Yes, I liked sucking your cock." Her voice was hoarse, her hips undulating beneath his attentions. "I wouldn't have done it if I didn't."

"No, I don't think you would have," he agreed, pulling away just long enough to look at her. She protested, her hands sliding down to tangle in his hair. "I doubt very much that you do anything you don't want to do."

"I don't." She raised her hips. "God, go back to what you were doing."

"Hmm." He hummed against her, and the vibrations traveled to her belly, which was knotted tightly. "What part of it do you like, I wonder? The actual cock sucking? Or pleasing your partner?"

She parted her lips, trying to gather her thoughts enough to formulate an answer, but it seemed that his question was rhetorical. He pressed his mouth to her flesh again, but this time it was with an intensity that stole her breath.

When she'd flirted with him earlier, at her shop, she'd thought she would have to be the one to seduce him. The one to convince a man in a suit to take a walk on the wild side.

As he slid a finger inside her and continued to circle her clit with his tongue, she admitted that she wasn't the one doing the seducing. And she was just fine with that.

"Fuck, yes." He flicked his tongue over her clit, and she felt the shock of sensation all the way to her toes. "Right there. More."

"Greedy girl." He chuckled as she tried to close her legs to get away from the sensation, and at the same time arched her hips to meet his mouth. "I like it."

Pulling his finger out of her slippery folds, he surged back in, this time with two. He scissored them inside her, stretching her swollen tissues, and Beth felt the tension inside her start to coil tighter and tighter.

"That's it." He slapped her inner thigh again, right in the same place. The skin there was starting to burn, in the best possible way. It heightened the pleasure that was threatening to break. "You're going to come for me, right now. If you do, then I'll give you my cock."

"God." No, this man certainly didn't need to be seduced. The more she writhed against him, the filthier that look on his face got. It was like he'd been covered in a fine sheen of ice—colorless and tasteless, it had still only given her an impression of the man beneath. His orgasm had shattered that ice, and now she was getting glimpses of the full thing.

The real thing.

And she liked it.

She ached to see it all.

"Come on." He scraped his teeth over her clit again, and the wave inside her rose higher and higher. "Let go."

He crooked the two fingers inside her, rubbing them over a spot that made her see stars. At the same time he used his other hand to rub roughly over the skin he'd smacked, reigniting the burn. It was that burn that made the wave finally crest. Beth cried out, Ford's name tumbling from her lips as she shook around him, grinding her face into his mouth.

He licked her through the shudders, sending her reeling into an aftershock. When the waves finally ebbed, she lay back on the bed panting, a sheen of sweat trying to cool her feverish skin.

"You're awfully good at that."

"She wiped a hand over her brow.

"I'm good at lots of things." He stood, and she struggled to prop herself up on her limp arms so that she could see him. He stood at the end of the bed with his shirt open, his pants around his hips and intent in his eyes.

It was a good look.

She watched, her mouth dry, as he peeled the shirt away from that defined chest. It fell to the floor as he hooked his hands in the waistband of his suit pants, slowly pulling them down. His cock, now fully erect again, popped free, and she couldn't help but suck in a breath.

Most men stripped themselves out of their clothes as fast as possible. She usually did the same, so she'd never found cause to complain. It had never even occurred to her that watching a man disrobe could be so hot.

Ford knew exactly what he was doing to her. He knew just how good he looked. And damn if the arrogance on his face wasn't hot as hell.

He let his pants fall to the floor, kicking them to

the side. He stood there completely naked, smirking as she looked her fill.

Yeah, he knew she liked what she saw.

"You look awfully pleased with yourself," she managed to pant as she crawled backward on the bed. She swallowed hard when he placed one knee, then the other, on the bed. He closed the distance between them quickly, and she expected him to range his lean body out on top of hers. Instead he placed his hands on her shoulders, stroked them down to cup her breasts. She arched into the touch, rising up on her knees to offer herself to him.

"I've just made a sexy woman scream my name," he replied, rubbing his thumbs over her nipples with a soft touch that only made her crave more. "What's not to be pleased about?"

He caught her piercing in the fingers of one hand, rolling it. The pleasure snapped through her as he explored the silver bar, growling out a sound of pleasure that told her how much he liked it.

"I'm going to play with this more later," he promised, dipping his head to run his tongue over the bar and her nipple in one slow lick. Then with swift movements, he released her breasts, sliding his hands down to her waist. Grasping the soft curves tightly, he rolled her, settling himself with his back to the headboard. Her knees were on either side of his, straddling his lap, and she gasped as her wet, swollen cleft pressed against his erection.

"I'll be more pleased when you ride my cock." His voice was low enough that she had to duck her head to hear him.

"I like the way you talk to me." God, did she ever. It made her hotter, wetter than she could ever remember being.

Something sparked in the brown of those wraith-like eyes, and she responded to it. Lifting her arms, she looped them around his neck, and she watched as his stare tracked along the colorful ink that ran from her wrists to her shoulders.

"Why have you chosen to mark yourself like this?" She stiffened for a moment, but there was no censure in his voice. Just curiosity. It made her relax. She truly didn't care if other people didn't like her ink, but it still pissed her off when they judged her for it.

Yes, she had tattoos. She also had a brain. A family. A business. The ink on her skin was just one small part of her.

Ford wasn't judging her, though she'd bet her non-existent funds that he'd never been so up close and personal with inked skin before.

"Two reasons." Her voice was husky, and she paused to clear her throat. "First. My sister Amy is a tattoo artist. When she started getting into it, my sisters and I were all drawn toward marking things that are important to us on our skin. Claiming it, I guess."

Releasing him with one hand, she trailed her newly free fingers over her oldest tattoo, which slithered across her left forearm. It read Music Soothes the Savage Beast. She'd gotten it at eighteen, when she'd been full of emotions she didn't understand and the only thing that had assuaged them were the hours that she spent at the battered old piano in their house.

It had been almost ten years, but the words still fit.

"And second?" He sank his teeth into her lower lip, sending a thrill through her veins. Almost like he knew what she was about to say.

"Second?" Planting a hand on his chest, she dug her nails in, just the tiniest bit. He hissed, but the wildness on his face told her he liked it.

"Second is that I liked the pain."

He exhaled, something that sounded like a curse word but wasn't fully coherent. He seemed to be struggling with himself again, with that need that he didn't seem to want to fully acknowledge.

She couldn't have said if the need in his eyes meant he'd won or he'd lost. She knew which side she was coming out on, though, when he nipped at her lip again, this time sinking his teeth in hard enough that she knew the soft curve would be swollen tomorrow.

"That shouldn't be so hot," he muttered, closing his eyes and tipping his head back. She took advantage of the moment to trace her tongue down the column of his throat. He shuddered.

"Why are you lying to yourself?" Studying the cords of his neck, she licked her lips, then sank her teeth into the spot where they met his shoulder. He reared up beneath her, his cock sliding through the slickness of her folds and grinding against her clit. "You like it, too. As long as we're both into it, what's wrong with that?"

He didn't answer, at least not with words. Instead his hands found her hips, squeezing before delivering a sharp slap to each side. The heat spread beneath his fingers, and she rubbed her taut nipples against his chest in response. Her piercing caught on his skin, making her shudder.

"Yeah, like that." He wasn't even inside her yet, and she could feel the pleasure rising. "Feels so good."

He cursed again, under his breath, but didn't argue. He agreed without words, slapping her hips again, then rubbing roughly over the heated skin.

She ground down against him, savoring the tease of his hard length against her wetness. She was reaching a fever pitch.

"I want you to do it now," he growled into her ear. "Sit on me. Now."

It was on the tip of her tongue to tease him, to glide back and forth over his rigid cock to show him who was really in control here.

The look in his eyes told her that the time for playing was over. Her pulse sped, and something dark and needy started to gather in a tangle in the depths of her belly.

"Condom?" She spoke against his lips, then sank into the kiss when he pulled at her hair and held her in place. Little nerve endings sparked along her scalp. And she couldn't hold back a purr of satisfaction.

He'd been listening, and he was giving her what she wanted. What she craved. Every minute that they were together, skin on skin, seemed to bring out more and more of the beast inside him.

She was dying to see what he would be like if that creature escaped.

"My pants pocket." He didn't let go until she tore herself away, crawling across the bed to reach for the suit pants he'd left on the floor. When she was bent over, rummaging in the pockets, he took the opportunity to rain three quick spanks down on her ass, all on one side, and she reared back, gasping.

"Yes." She hissed it out between her teeth as wetness surged in her cleft.

Grabbing her by the waist, he hauled her back to the head of the bed, again situating her across his lap. She reached for the condom, and he held it up to her lips. Grinning, she caught it in her teeth, biting tight. He pulled and the foil ripped. She plucked out the latex ring and, pinching the tip, pulled his cock away from where it rested against his belly and rolled the sheath down to the root.

A low growl of satisfaction slipped from his lips at

her touch, and his hips rose from the bed. His movements became bossy—bossier—and within seconds he had her positioned over his cock, the head nestled between her lower lips.

"Take me." It was an order, one that made her melt. She sank down just enough to take the tip inside her, meaning to consume him slowly. He had other ideas, his hands driving her down so that he impaled her in one hard thrust. She cried out, rocking on top of him, both trying to get away and to get closer.

"You're tight." He grunted beneath her as he gave a series of short thrusts, trying to work the rest of the way inside her. She couldn't catch her breath—Jesus, but he was big. "Open for me, baby."

She wasn't sure she could. They rocked for a moment, her body fighting him but wanting more pleasure. Claiming her lips, he slid his hand from her hip around her backside, sliding between her legs from behind to tease at her full folds.

Slickness surged. She moaned, rocking on him, and he sank in another impossible inch. Her fingers grabbed at his shoulders, searching for purchase.

He returned his hand to her hip, pulling her bodily up. His thick cock dragged over her tight and now incredibly sensitive inner walls, sparking nerve endings with every pulse.

"That's it." He worked her back down, and she felt that storm of pleasure gathering again. When he spanked her hip again, she felt herself melting into something dark and dreamy, more decadent than she'd ever felt before.

"Ford." She wasn't a beggar. Usually. Right now all she wanted was for the sensations to continue. To grow.

She rocked back and forth on his lap, had the pleasure of watching his own expression grow hazy. His stare caught hers, intense and sure, and she found that she couldn't look away. That look was her anchor in the intensity she felt as he guided her up and down.

It was too intense. A tendril of affection unfurled in her chest, and it would have made her panic if she had room left to feel anything else at all.

She started to squirm, desperate for the release that remained just out of reach. His eyes, his hands on her hips grounded her, and her breath started to come in pants.

"Ride me." He trailed a hand up her back, tracing her spine before tangling in her hair yet again. She didn't know why she liked that so much from him, but every little tug had her growing even wetter. "Take what you need. Do it now."

When he commanded her like that, she couldn't have done anything else. Sinking her teeth into her lower lip, she centered her weight on her knees, her palms splayed out on his broad, hard chest.

Slowly, she rose, shuddering at the pleasure. As wet as she was, she still had to work her way back down, the sting melting into need with the delicious drag of his cock over her inner walls.

The way they fit together, the connection that snapped in the air between them, God, just the way he held so perfectly still, letting her do as he'd told her to—to ride him. It all mixed together into a tangled knot of pleasure that was sending her higher than she'd ever been. She'd meant to keep her movements slow, deliberate—to savor the climb to what she knew would be one of the best releases of her life.

She couldn't be slow. Her movements quickened until she was rocking back and forth on his cock with abandon, grinding her clit against the solid planes of his abs. He couldn't seem to remain still anymore, either. One of his hands was digging into her hip, urging her to move faster. His pelvis rose up every time she slammed down, and they both shuddered every time he bottomed out inside her.

Her body started to shake. She was so close, and it was like she'd been caught in the wake of a tsunami—she was powerless to do anything but be pulled wherever the storm wanted to go.

Back slamming into the headboard, he ground up into her so hard that she saw stars. The bite of pain was a crimson ribbon snapping through her, and the storm inside her started to break.

With a growl, he slid a hand up to grasp her breast. She arched into his palm, crying out when he rubbed a thumb teasingly over her pierced nipple.

She needed more than that. As though she'd said it aloud, he tightened his hold until he was tugging lightly. She felt the pull all the way down to her core, and when he tugged again, her entire body snapped.

"Ford!" She hadn't meant to say his name, but it spilled from her lips as her orgasm broke. Clinging to his shoulders, she rode the edge of her release, crying out again when he tugged on her nipple one last time, sending an aftershock coursing through her.

"You have no idea how good that feels." She could tell from his ragged breaths and the sweat beading his forehead that he was close. She stared down at that gorgeous face, fascinated as it contorted with pleasure yet retained the fierceness that had sharpened with every little bit that he'd let go. "I can feel every ripple of your pleasure. Pleasure that I gave to you."

With most men she would make some kind of pithy comment at that, something along the lines of being able to pleasure herself just as well as they could, but here and now, that would have been a lie. A big one.

She'd had some good sex before. Great sex, even. But this? This was something on an entirely new level.

"You gave me this," she moaned softly into his ear, still writhing against him even though she was losing control of her muscles. "Let me give you what you want."

He groaned, a wrenching sound like he was in pain. Deliberately, she clenched around him, and his breath caught. Beth thought it was the sexiest thing she'd ever heard—this big, powerful man brought out of his mind with pleasure because of her.

"Fuck." He ground the word out between clenched teeth, and Beth felt him swell inside her. She gasped as he thrust several times—hard, choppy pulses as he found his own release.

Out of breath, she dipped her head, intending to rest her cheek on his shoulder. Instead, he lifted a hand and pressed it to her cheek, guiding her so that her forehead rested against his, her eyes looking into his own. It was more intimate than she should have been comfortable with, but as the endorphins flooded her system and left her completely blissed out, it felt strangely right.

She waited until he closed his eyes to close hers, still straddling him with his cock inside her. He'd claimed her entirely—in this moment, her body was his.

She'd think about that more later, but now, she let herself float away.

CHAPTER SIX

ANTICIPATION AND APPREHENSION tightened in Ford's gut as he walked the short distance from his motel to the garage, inhaling deep mouthfuls of the apple and smoke air of an early afternoon in fall. A few minutes ago he'd slung his laptop bag over his shoulder and looked around the small cube of his motel room. The sheets were on the floor, the pillows tossed halfway across the room. The heavy musk of sex was in the air, along with lingering hints of engine grease and vanilla.

It had made lust surge to his groin. Hell, he'd been half-hard since he'd woken up at four in the morning and turned to Beth, hungry for another helping of her body.

He'd gone hungry, because she'd been gone. He was normally a light sleeper, but after that insane orgasm he must have slept like the dead, allowing her to sneak out.

It was just as well. They'd both gotten what they'd wanted—some incredible sex.

The memory of her on her knees in front of him, his cock in her mouth as she let him boss her around, wasn't one he would soon forget. The way she'd responded to him, had urged him to let his dominance out, would be burned in his brain for a long time, even if it was something he should probably forget.

They'd had fun, but he still felt the stirrings of shame. He'd been rough with her—had pulled her hair, spanked her, played endlessly with that fascinating piercing of hers.

Nice men didn't do that. He supposed he should think of it like a diet. He'd cheated a little, had a serving of rich, sinful chocolate cake. Now it was time to go back to chicken and steamed veggies.

Was he really comparing sex to a bland meal? As he reached the end of the garage's driveway, he forced himself to chuckle. He liked the sex he usually had.

He liked chicken and veggies.

Not the same as cake, though.

He shook his head to clear his thoughts. What the hell was wrong with him? He'd never felt awkward during a morning after, probably because he usually only slept with nice women he was dating.

He'd never felt like this after sex. He wasn't sure what to do with it.

He paused at the end of the driveway, adjusting the strap of his laptop bag on his shoulder. Irritated by the state of his car, he hadn't paid that much attention to the structure the last time he'd been here. Now he took in the large gardens, the wide expanse of grassy lawns—probably a bitch to keep up. In fact, both were looking pretty neglected. As was the house, two stories and spacious but covered in weathered brown wood, the roof sagging and missing shingles.

Still, his hotelier eye looked over it all and saw good bones. The house had once been something special, and he wondered how Beth had become a part of it. She'd mentioned sisters, but apart from that and the garage, he knew nothing about her.

He had no business wanting to know more about her. She wasn't the kind of woman he got involved with.

He'd never let go like he had last night. Real men shouldn't want the kind of things he'd let himself do, and yet he couldn't help his mouth watering with the hunger for more.

Get a grip, man.

Ford scowled at himself and started up the driveway. On the short walk here he'd passed several men begging at the side of the road, and more than a few businesses that were shuttered, even gutted and tagged with spray paint. It was clearly not a wealthy area of Boston. It was such a stark contrast to his plush waterfront condo that he'd felt the stirrings of guilt, but he shoved them away.

He'd worked hard for what he had. Why should he feel bad about it?

But did that mean that the people who lived here didn't work hard? Before yesterday he might have actually made that generalization, but after seeing the operation that Beth ran, he knew that at least one resident of this area was hardworking.

Chirpy pop music blasted from the open garage this time. Man, her music taste was strange. Though when he cocked his head, he thought he recognized the song—from where, he had no idea. Yeah, one of those songs by that British boy band with all the hair.

Heavy metal. Sitar music. Boy banders in skinny jeans. Just a few more pieces in the puzzle that was Beth.

The bubbly music hid the female voices until he was framed by the garage door. He stopped short when he saw the three women lounging there, none of whom were Beth.

"Well, well." One of the woman pushed herself out of the ratty lawn chair she'd been sitting in, reaching for an open can of soda on one of the workbenches. She was tall and slender, with long blond curls that fell to her waist. Her torn jeans and white tank top revealed a fair amount of skin, and most of that skin was covered in ink—she even had a tattoo covering her collarbone and throat, one that looked like a lacy collar. At least twice as much ink as Beth. He wondered if this was Amy, the tattoo artist sister. "You need some directions there, honey?"

Honey?

"Easy, Ames." One of the other women was reclining in an old, torn armchair. Ford blinked when he looked at her—he couldn't help it. She was beautiful, even in denim overalls with—wow.

She was wearing overalls over just a bra, leaving her generous curves on more than full display. And she was knitting. He didn't know where to look.

"Why easy?" The first woman took a couple of steps in his direction, and he suspected that the sway to her hips was deliberate. "Maybe the lost little puppy is looking for a...meal."

Ford knew that he wasn't misinterpreting the double entendre.

"Because," the knitting woman started, smiling calmly up at Ford, "I bet this is what kept our Beth out of the house till all hours."

Setting down her knitting, she brushed pink-streaked chestnut hair back, pulling it up into a ponytail. Then she stretched, causing her curves to spill out of her overalls. She had some kind of tattoo stretching out of her cleavage.

The third woman said nothing, just beat her heels on the workbench she was sitting on. Average height, she had the leanest build of the sisters, emphasized by the skinny, ripped jeans and tight men's T-shirt that she wore. Her hair was cut in a sharp bob dyed inky black that brushed along a chiseled jawline and slightly pointed chin as she kicked.

Her caramel-colored eyes were fixed on Ford with more than a little suspicion.

"Mmm." The first woman, the blonde one—Amy?—looked Ford over slowly, and damned if she didn't make him squirm. "Interesting choice this time, Beth."

"I thought so. And he has a name. It's Ford." Without warning, Beth pushed herself out from beneath the clunky gray SUV that sat in the garage. Ford jolted—he'd been keeping an eye on the other women and hadn't noticed her work boots at his feet. Lying on her back on that rolling thing she used, she looked up at him with those intense eyes of hers, a small smirk playing around the corners of her lips. "Hello."

"Hi." Seeing her spread out there like that, beneath him, had interest stirring anew. He'd wanted to take her like that when he'd woken up in the early morning—to roll between her soft thighs and slide into her while she was sleepy and submissive.

He didn't like that she'd run out without saying goodbye. It must have shown on his face, some sign of his displeasure, because her posture changed, just ever so slightly, responding to him.

She ran her tongue over her lips, stare still fastened on his, and he remembered the way she'd looked when she'd ridden his cock—pure sex.

He wanted her again. Now.

"Found what you were looking for?" The woman in the bra and overalls picked up her knitting again, smirking at him over the top of it. The other two women laughed.

That was enough of that. Ford was never intimidated. He wouldn't let himself be now. Wordlessly, he extended a hand to Beth. With a bemused smile, she took it, seemingly entertained by the way the other women were talking to him.

When she was on her feet, she tugged to pull her hand away. He held tight, drawing her in closer, until there was only a ribbon of space between their bodies. Her eyes widened as heat passed between them, and he heard her soft exhale as he dipped his head.

"Thanks for last night," he whispered into her ear. A strand of purple had fallen loose of her braid, and he tucked it behind her ear, making sure that his lips grazed her cheek as she leaned back, savoring her small shudder.

What the hell was he doing? Looking for round two? What else could he want?

She arched an eyebrow at him, as if to ask if he was quite done, but when his gaze lowered, he saw that her nipples had bunched up tightly and were pressing against her thin T-shirt, under which she seemed to be naked. He couldn't hold back the smirk. She pressed her lips together and turned to the other women.

"Meet my sisters. The one hitting on you is

Amy—she's the tattoo artist I mentioned. The one knitting is Meg, and the one sitting on the workbench is Jo." She gestured to each with a hand as she introduced them. Amy licked her lips. Meg smiled sweetly. Jo scowled.

He had no idea what to make of the lot of them.

"Your car is ready." Reaching into the pocket of the coveralls that she'd tied at the waist, she fished out his key ring, dangled it in front of him. She followed it with a total scribbled on a Post-it note. "Will that be cash or card? I don't take checks."

Last night he'd tasted her on his tongue, and now she was demanding that he pay up for the work she'd done. He wasn't put off—hell, no. He was a businessman.

It was sexy as hell.

"Credit will be fine." He didn't bother looking at the total. Handing her his card, he watched as she took it to her bench and ran it through one of the old-fashioned imprint devices. Her sister Jo nudged her with her foot, and when Beth looked up something wordless passed between them, ending only when Beth rolled her eyes.

Ford tracked her progress back to him. She was surprisingly graceful, even in the baggy coveralls and chunky boots. It reminded him of the way she'd moved last night, and his body tightened.

Her eyes darkened, and he knew that she'd noticed. A pulse passed between them.

Having sex hadn't caused the fire between them to burn out—no, it had stoked the flame. His focus narrowed until he saw nothing but her, the vanilla and grease scent now conditioned in him to make him hard.

"Didn't get enough the first round?" Her words were barely audible, a whisper against his lips. She hooked her index fingers in his belt loops, and awareness of the sexual tension between them was painted all over her face.

"You left before I was done with this tight little body of yours." Surely if he'd had another taste—or two—he wouldn't be craving her again so strongly now.

She smiled up at him, but her eyes narrowed. "Maybe I was done with you."

"I don't think so." Not with the way she was vibrating against him right now. So why had she left?

"Lunchtime, girls!" Another woman entered the garage, opening a worn wooden door that he thought probably led to the house. Of average height, she had birch-brown hair pulled back into a messy bun, with a striking streak of white at her right temple. She was wearing cutoff jeans that had faded to almost white, an equally well-worn T-shirt that boasted a silkscreen of a palm tree and a long, loose kimono-type garment with an earthy orange-and-white pattern. She looked directly at him, arching an eyebrow over a pair of bright blue eyes that looked exactly like Beth's.

"Who are you?" The question wasn't accusing, but still he felt compelled to answer.

"I'm...a customer of Beth's." He winced inwardly as he spoke, knowing that Beth wouldn't care for that description. Her expression didn't change, however, and he found that part of him didn't like that.

"He's where Beth was all night, Mamesie." Jo slid off the bench, casting him a challenging look. Wow, these women didn't give an inch.

"Given the way he's got his hands on my daughter, I gathered that," said the older woman. She smiled at him. "Well, he can come for lunch as well."

"Uh..." He didn't know how to respond to the unexpected offer. Beth released his belt loops as he stepped back. A derisive noise came from Jo.

The older woman—Mamesie—hummed as she looked him up and down. He found himself standing straighter under her eyes.

"Do you eat lunch?"

"Yes." He knew where she was going with this.

"Were you planning to eat lunch today?"

"Yes." His throat felt tight. Beth fascinated him. He still wanted her. But lunch with her family?

He didn't do that.

"Well, then you can eat lunch with us." Mamesie gestured for them all to follow her. Amy and Meg did immediately, but Jo lingered on the steps, watching him. When she was sure that he was looking back, she pointed at her own eyes with two fingers, then at him to indicate she was watching him.

He felt like he was caught in a windstorm, being pulled along through no decision of his own.

What the hell? He planted his feet. He was a millionaire. He owned a very successful chain of hotels. He didn't do things that he didn't want to do. He would just wait until the rest of the women had headed into the house, then get in his car and go. That was what he'd planned to do anyway, wasn't it?

Beth crossed her arms over her chest. A knowing smile curved her lips—one that said she'd expected him to do just this.

That was why she'd left in the middle of the night—she'd wanted to beat him to the punch.

That didn't sit right with him. Besides, something about this woman fascinated him. Yeah, he didn't do family stuff, but it wasn't like she was expecting him to, right? Where was the harm? They both knew this wasn't a long-term deal. That didn't mean he had to pretend that he wasn't interested in her, which he most certainly was.

"All right." He enjoyed the look of surprise that crossed her face. "What's for lunch?"

CHAPTER SEVEN

THE LAST THING Beth had expected was for Ford to accept Mamesie's invitation to lunch, and she really didn't know what to think about it. He hadn't needed much convincing, either, which surprised the hell out of her. A guy like him—she didn't expect him to do family stuff.

Nothing about their opposites attract–style hookup was normal, so she supposed that lunch with her family while her body was still sore from the way he'd used it the night before wasn't that weird.

Still, she felt apprehension as she led the way into the house—not a common emotion for her. She wasn't ashamed of her home, not at all, but as she and Ford followed her mother and sisters into the well-worn house, she tracked his gaze, seeing things through his eyes.

When her dad had been alive, they'd had money. Not a ton of it, or they probably would have lived in a different part of the city, but they'd had enough to keep the house in good repair.

Then her dad had died overseas. He'd always been the primary source of income for the house—Mamesie made good money on her pottery when she sold it, but an artist's income was sporadic. Over the years they'd found ways to make the house their own on a budget, and the result was cluttered and cozy.

Beth liked to think of it as bohemian, but she suspected that when Ford looked at the scarves pinned to the walls, the worn rugs layered on the floors, the tables full of scented candles, he saw junk.

Didn't matter, she reminded herself. He wasn't the one who lived here.

"Mamesie's made soup." Pushing away that thought, Beth made a show of sniffing the air. "You're lucky. She makes the best soup in the South End."

"What's that other smell?" Coming up beside her in the tight hallway, Ford inhaled deeply. Beth ignored the sparks that danced over her skin as his pelvis brushed against the round curves of her ass. "Is it citrus?"

"Lemongrass." Beth gestured to a small diffuser that sat on a table. She was pleased with his comment, since the scent was her favorite. "Mamesie changes the oil in it depending on her mood."

"Smells great." He sniffed again, and she just blinked at him. The comment was not what she expected from the terse, tense man who'd stormed into her garage yesterday. She'd thought she had Ford

Lassiter figured out, but it seemed like maybe she was wrong.

Unbidden, something fluttered in her midsection.

"Amy, Jo, set the table." When Beth led Ford into the cozy area that held the living room and dining room, they found Mamesie with brightly quilted oven mitts on, carrying a large pot of steaming soup from the kitchen. Setting it on the scarred wooden table, she wiped the sweat from her forehead with the sleeve of her kimono. "Meg, you get the bread. Beth, why don't you play us a little something while they set the table?"

"Play something?" Ford turned to Beth, surprise evident on his face. She couldn't help the quick, bright streak of pleasure at being asked to play.

Holding up her hands, she wiggled her fingers, smirking. "These babies are good for more than one thing."

His expression darkened, heated, and Beth felt an answering tangle of warmth tightening in her gut as she thought about how it had felt to have her hands on his body.

"Beth?" Mamesie cast her an exasperated look, and Beth flushed, just a bit. She and her sisters were open about their sexuality, and they'd learned it from their mother, but there were still some boundaries. She wasn't about to cross one now by jumping on Ford here in the living room, no matter how much the man could turn her on with a single look.

"What are we in the mood for, girls?" Gesturing Ford to the threadbare sofa draped in brightly patterned blankets, she crossed the room to her old but very well-loved piano. It had been a vintage piece, a garage sale find, when her father had purchased it for decoration, and now it was ancient. Beth had fallen in love with it at first sight, prompting their dad to sign them all up for lessons. Meg, Jo and Amy could plunk out a simple melody, but Beth was the one with the passion.

"What was it that you played a couple of nights ago?" Amy asked as she set mismatched silverware on the table. "That one by Sarah somebody?"

"'Sweet Ones,'" Beth answered as she ran her fingers lightly over the keys. "Sarah Slean."

Her breathing slowed as she seated herself on the bench. It was solid wood, but it was so comfortable for her that she swore the years had molded it to her curves.

The fluttering she'd felt at having Ford in her home eased, her world centering as she placed her fingers on the necessary keys.

She could feel Ford's eyes burning into her from behind as she started to play, but within a moment she was drawn completely into the music. Her body moved as she played, and sweat beaded on her brow—she'd always been an energetic musician. The energy that filled her demanded it, though, and when the cover song she was playing ended she segued right into another, one that she'd written herself that matched the tempo of the first song.

Coaxing the last notes from the battered instrument, she inhaled deeply, folding her hands in her lap.

"Nice one, Beth!" Amy hooted from behind her. "Did you write that?"

"I did." An uncharacteristic hint of shyness colored her words. She knew that she could play, was talented, even. But while she never minded playing one of her own compositions for her family, she rarely felt confident enough in their strength to play them for anyone else.

They were a part of her, something she'd given birth to. Someone could hate her tattoos, her hair, but if they hated her music, it would hurt.

Stretching for something to do with her arms, she twisted to look at Ford. He looked slightly taken aback, and she held her breath until he spoke.

"You're very talented." His tone indicated that she'd impressed him, and warmth suffused her. She shouldn't have cared about his opinion—she barely knew him—but she liked to at least try to be honest with herself. There was something here between them. Something more than sex. They were so different that she really didn't think it was going to go anywhere, but that didn't turn off the interest rising inside her.

She liked that she'd impressed him. Liked that he was here, in her home.

"Thanks." Rising from the piano bench, she sauntered across one of the worn rugs until she stood directly in front of him, her knees brushing against his own. His stare traveled the length of her body with intent, lighting her up from inside, and she sucked in a breath.

"Why aren't you doing something with your talent?" Her pulse skipped a beat when he took one of her hands and studied the faint smears of grease that never seemed to come off. "Why work as a mechanic when you can do something so fantastic?"

What?

Both flattered and stung, she tugged her hand back. He'd unknowingly just aired her deepest dream. The one that her life would never allow. "I like my job. I'm good at it."

"But—"

She shook her head, cutting him off again. She didn't want to talk about this. Thinking about what she really wanted hurt. "How would I make a living at playing the piano? A few bucks here and there while I chased gigs at restaurants full of snooty people? I need a steadier paycheck than that."

He didn't seem convinced, so she continued. "And like I said, I like what I do. I have passion for it."

It was true. She loved cars, loved picking them apart to discover what was needed to make them run again. She was good with her hands, and this was one more way to use them. "Isn't there more than one thing that you love?"

"No." Ford pulled back a bit, and puzzlement was clear on his face. She wasn't entirely sure that he was understanding what she was saying. "No, I really just work. My company is my life."

"That's sad." Stepping back, she led the way to the table, but he'd confused her as much as she'd confused him. He'd said that his company was his life, and she was inclined to believe him. But how could he live that way? Didn't he have a hobby? Friends? Something more than casual sex with a near stranger?

She didn't think he would appreciate it if he knew, but his words made her heart ache. He had what appeared to be a boatload of cash, but what good was it if all he did was work for more?

They were so different. And yet when they sat down beside each other at the table, and their hands brushed, something sizzled inside her. Beside her Ford shifted in awareness, and she felt her pulse quicken.

They were different, and yet that connection—that sexual tension—was undeniable.

She was willing to see where it could go. She wondered if he would be, too.

"Soup's up," Mamesie said. Beth busied herself by passing the pot to Ford first, since he was the guest.

She watched him ladle some of Mamesie's Italian wedding soup into a green glazed-pottery bowl. She liked watching his hands, liked remembering what they'd done to her body.

"So. Ford, right?" Meg took the pot next, serving herself into a bowl of cherry red. "You must be rich."

"Margaret Marchande." Mamesie spoke sharply from the head of the table. "You're being rude."

Meg shrugged, grinning. "We're all wondering, with that Turbo sitting in the garage. That suit you're wearing. Though it looks a bit rumpled, hmm, Beth?"

Beth rolled her eyes. "Meg's obsessed with how the other half lives. Your half, I guess I should say."

Ford arched an eyebrow as he spooned up some soup and made a noise of pleasure. He didn't seem put off by the question. "I am wealthy, yes. I own a chain of hotels."

"What are you doing with our Beth, then?" Jo's words were more than a bit aggressive, but Beth was pleased that Ford barely blinked at her sister's sharp tone.

"I—"

"I think we know what he's doing with Beth." Amy cut him off, and Beth was disappointed that she didn't get to hear what he was going to say. Her youngest sister grinned over her own bowl of soup, and Beth frowned back at her. They all shared the same open attitude about sex, and they weren't shy about details with one another, either. But Amy's words stung a little.

Did her sisters really think it was impossible that a man like Ford would want to be with a woman like Beth for more than just sex? What the hell?

Underneath the table, Ford settled his hand on her thigh, squeezing gently. She wasn't sure if it was because he'd sensed her upset and was trying to soothe her, or because he'd craved the touch, but when his hand slid a few inches higher, she felt her breath hitch.

She'd thought that one time would be enough. But here she was, need gathering hot and tight for him again.

"I think that's enough of the grand inquisition." Pushing away her half-empty bowl, Beth stood. She wanted another taste of this man, and she wanted it now.

Ford had just finished his soup as well, so she stacked his bowl with hers, then tugged at his sleeve to get him moving. "Come on."

"Thank you for the hospitality." Ford nodded at Mamesie before Beth was able to tug him from the room. That he took the time to thank her mother did something funny to her insides.

Without another word, she pulled him from the room, ignoring her sisters' knowing laughter that followed her.

CHAPTER EIGHT

FORD FOLLOWED BETH'S curves back out of the garage like she was a piper and he was dancing to her tune. When he'd placed a hand on her thigh, he'd wanted her attention, but he hadn't expected her to all but melt into the touch.

She was so fucking sexy. No other woman had ever gotten him hot like this.

He paused just outside the door that divided the house from the garage. He wanted to just look at her, to try to analyze why her hair, her ink, her devil-may-care attitude got to him the way that it did.

He watched as she sauntered to the front of his Turbo. His pulse stuttered when she undid the knot she'd made at the waist of her coveralls. They fell to the stained concrete floor, leaving him with a killer view of her sweet ass in insanely tight little shorts.

This. This was why she was so sexy—her unapologetic hunger. The way she wasn't afraid to get down and dirty, to push him to do the same.

The need to grab that tight little ass, to darken it

with his palm the way he had the night before, was nearly impossible to contain.

Hitching herself up onto the hood, Beth fisted her hands in the hem of her thin T-shirt. Tearing it up and over her head, she tossed it aside, then tugged the elastic from her messy braid. Inky black and violet rioted over her shoulders as she settled back onto her elbows, parting her thighs.

The silver bar nestled in one of her taut nipples glinted. Her breasts looked heavy and full, ready for his mouth. And when his gaze strayed between those sweet thighs, he saw that the crotch of those little shorts she was wearing was already damp.

"Fuck." He was off the stairs and to her before he could take his next breath. He put his hands on her knees and spread her legs farther, dipping his head to inhale her sweet scent.

"That's the idea, Sir Lassiter." She stretched out the *sir* on that velvet tongue of hers, and pure lust rocketed straight to his cock. "Fuck me. Now."

"Bossy little woman." Lifting his head, he feasted his gaze on those luscious tits. Needing to touch, he slid his hands up to cup them, catching the ripe nipples between forefingers and thumbs. She arched beneath the touch, falling back onto the hood of the car. Hooking her legs around his hips, she pulled his aching erection against her barely covered core, moaning when she rubbed over him.

He was going to have her again. Fuck, he needed

to have her again. He braced his hands on the cool metal on either side of her, dipping his head to nip at her neck. "The garage door is open."

"So it is." She rocked her hips against him, and he saw stars. "In a few minutes, you're going to be fucking me hard, right here on your pricey little car. And anyone could walk by and see. Anyone at all."

Fuck, fuck, but that turned him on even more. He knew he had a bit of an exhibitionist streak, but he tried not to look at it too hard.

Right now, with her dirty words and her tight little body, she was urging him to grab that desire that he tried to deny with both hands. Demanding that he own up to his dirty side.

Cupping her breasts in her hands, she began to play with those tits of hers, undulating when she pulled on her piercing. His last shreds of sanity fled.

"I hope someone walks by." If he was going to do this, then he was going to do it right. Grabbing her just above the knees, he hauled her down the car's hood until her ass rested on the front edge. She gasped at the sudden movement, but the groan that followed it told him she was right there with him. "Undo my pants."

"Gladly." Extending her arms, she worked the button at his waist free, then slowly—maddeningly—lowered his zipper. Those wicked fingers of hers brushed against his rigid length, and he hissed at the sensation.

"Pull me out." She stroked down his length again, fingers teasing him through the thin cotton of his boxer briefs, and he delivered a sharp tap to her hip. "Now."

Working her hands inside his waistband, she circled his shaft, rubbing a thumb over the tip. He felt red-hot liquid bead beneath her touch as she tugged the elastic down beneath his erection.

He indulged himself with a look down at the length of her—naked breasts swollen and pink, dampness between her thighs, legs wrapped around his waist and hands in his pants.

So. Fucking. Hot.

She squealed when, without warning, he flipped her over. Pressing her hot body against the cool metal of the hood, he dragged the little scrap of spandex down around her knees. The fabric was tight, holding her legs together, which was just what he wanted.

Bending over, he covered her from behind. Even through the fabric of his shirt, he could feel her little vibrations of excitement. She was as into this as he was.

He pressed his weight down, trapping her against his car. Circling her wrists with his fingers, he pinned her against the sleek car, running his lips over the shell of her ear.

"You'd like it if someone came by, wouldn't you?" He gave one small thrust, rubbing his naked cock through her slick folds, and she laughed breathlessly, raising her ass for more contact. "What would turn you on the most?"

She parted her lips, but no sound came out. Her hot breath misted across the hood.

"Let me think." Rolling his hips forward again, he thrust through her slickness, and the feeling was so heady his entire body tightened. "A lot of men were watching you at the bar last night. Watching you dance, put on a show."

"They were," she agreed, rubbing back against him.

"I bet you'd just love it if some of those men were out for a walk right now. Maybe heading down the street on their lunch breaks." Beneath him she whimpered. "They hear that sexy little sound that you just made and come to see what's going on."

She rose up on her toes, pushing back against him.

"Yeah, I can just picture it." He could. "Five or six men, crowding into the garage. The noises that they hear, they wonder if maybe someone is hurt. Instead they see that hot little tease from the bar last night. She's bent over the hood of a car in her own garage, and she's about to get fucked."

"Oh my God," Beth hissed out between her teeth. "Please. Now."

He could see it in his mind's eye—the men that had watched her provocative dancing had wanted her. They wouldn't question their luck at the open garage door—they'd just enjoy the show.

Enjoy watching him fuck *this* woman. Him. Fuck Beth. The fact that it could actually happen, that someone could come along right now and watch them together, was the hottest thing he'd ever felt.

Jesus, who the hell was he? He'd never talked dirty like this. He'd wanted to, oh, hell yes, but the way he'd been raised, he'd always known he didn't want to be like his father. Didn't want to treat women like objects.

Was that was he was doing here?

Looking down at Beth, he took in her flushed skin, so hot in contrast with the sleek metal of his Turbo. She was stretched out for his pleasure, but there was no doubt in his mind that she was here because she wanted to be. Because it turned her on.

And so help him, but she demanded that he do what turned him on, too.

He couldn't hold back any longer.

Working his hand into one of his pockets, he pulled out the condom that he'd tucked there earlier. He hadn't been sure what to make of Beth's leaving in the night, but he'd have been lying to himself if he said he hadn't been hopeful.

Not wanting to take his other hand from her, he caught the foil packet in his teeth and pulled. The ring of latex fell onto her back, and he snatched it up, conceding that he needed both hands free to put it on.

"Yes." Her voice was raw. Dirty. "Hurry."

Pinching the tip, he rolled the condom down his

length, his own touch feeling good on his engorged flesh. Catching the swell of her hip in one hand, he slid his sheathed cock through her cheeks one final time. "Ready?"

She nodded frantically, hips rocking.

He dipped a hand between her legs. She gasped when he tucked two fingers inside, and he exhaled loudly. She was soaked, and hot, and more than ready for him. And if she felt this fucking good on his fingers, then she was going to feel like heaven on his dick.

Placing the swollen head of his cock at her entrance, he thrust. Her moan mingled with the strangled sound from his own throat as he surged in to the hilt.

"Yes." Her voice was ragged with need. Her fingers scrabbled at the cool metal for something to hold on to. Her channel tightened around him in a snug embrace, and he saw stars.

"Better be quiet," he muttered as he rocked his pelvis, his hips still flush against her gorgeous heart-shaped ass, "or someone will come in, will see what a dirty girl you are."

"I am," she agreed, rising up onto her toes. "I'm so dirty. And so are you."

Her words spurred something on in him. With a guttural sound, he placed one hand flat on her back and started to thrust in earnest, pulling out slowly, then surging back in. She met his thrusts as best she could in her position, a small sound of pure pleasure falling from her lips every time he hilted inside her.

Sensation coiled tightly inside him, and he knew he wasn't going to last long. Working his hand between Beth's soft abdomen and the hood of the car, he found her swollen clit. Catching it between his fingers, he rubbed. Her hips jumped as she absorbed the pleasure.

She clenched around him as she gasped through her climax, wringing his own release from him. He collapsed over her, trying to brace his weight as he pressed against her back so that he didn't crush her.

They were silent for a long moment, sweat and heat sealing them together. Beneath him, Beth laughed breathlessly.

"You've got some moves, Sir Lassiter." Sliding out from beneath him, she rolled those skimpy little shorts back up. Her skin was glossy, her cheeks flushed as she moved, completely comfortable in her nakedness.

"Jesus." Legs shaking, he tucked himself back into his pants, then raked a hand through his hair. He knew he'd never forget the sight of her, topless with legs spread on the hood of his Turbo. Daring him to take what he wanted. "What was that for?"

Retrieving her T-shirt, Beth tugged it back over her head, leaving the coveralls on the floor where they lay. That silver bar in her nipple pressed against the tissue-thin cotton, and he found he couldn't look away.

Heading to the small, rusty fridge that stood by the workbench, she pulled out two cans of Coke. Studying him with those bewitching blue eyes, she walked back and pressed one into his hand.

"I felt like it." She smirked up at him as she popped the top on her can and took a long drink.

"I'm never going to look at the Turbo the same way again." He was pretty sure they'd just incinerated some of his brain cells, and she confirmed it when she searched his face and laughed.

"That look on your face. You look like you just got laid for the first time." She took another sip, then licked her lips. "But maybe it's just one of the first times that you really let yourself go."

"I don't know how to answer that." Discomfited, he cracked open his own can, hoping the combination of sugar and caffeine would jolt him back to reality. The way she was looking at him—it felt like she could see right to his very soul, like she had full access to all of those dark needs and wants that he tried so hard to keep hidden away.

"Ford." Placing her can on the workbench, Beth laid one of her hands on his cheek. "I don't get it. Why are you fighting so hard against what you like when it's what you obviously want?"

Those damn witchy eyes of hers. He couldn't deny those needs when she was looking right at him like that. Jerking back, he turned away from her, chugging his Coke and trying to cool off.

When he turned back, she was still waiting, the slightest hint of mockery on her face. Like instead of thinking that he was more of a man for denying his kink, she believed he was less of one.

It pissed him right off.

"So what do you do when you're dating someone?" She seemed genuinely puzzled. "Who are you then?"

"I—" How the hell was he supposed to answer that? He dated. He dated a lot, but he knew that his wealth attracted a lot of women who only showed him their best side.

Just like he did. The parallel wasn't lost on him, but damn it. He didn't want to be thinking about this, didn't want to have to explain himself. He would not be like his father, treating women like crap.

No matter how much a purple-haired siren tempted him.

"I don't date women who are into…this." The words came out harsh, but he couldn't think straight. "And that's fine, because this isn't the real me."

"I see." Beth crossed her arms over her chest. "So it was someone else who just bent me over the hood of your car and fucked me where anyone could have seen?"

He winced, guilt and shame rising at her words.

He'd done just that. He'd treated her like an object. He was no better than his father.

"Gotcha." Her smile turning brittle, Beth sauntered over to her cluttered desk. Slamming a staple through a thin sheaf of paper, she crossed back to him and slapped it against his chest. "Here's your detailed service report. Have a nice day."

He took the paper, anger and something else warring inside him. She looked him over slowly, then snorted inelegantly.

"I feel sorry for you."

"What?" he sputtered, crumpling the report in his hands. "You're sorry for *me*?"

"Yup. It's a sad life you have if all you do is work and pretend to be someone you're not." She reached for her crumpled coveralls, and damn if his eyes weren't drawn to that freaking silver bar through her nipple. She noted the direction of his gaze and smirked.

"This isn't who I am." He crumpled the paper into a ball and threw it across the garage in frustration. "You bring this out in me!"

"Oh, no." She shook her head, her eyes emitting sapphire sparks. "Don't you blame me. This is who you are, Sir Lassiter. What you choose to do with it, though? That's up to you. But I'm not going to go along for the ride with someone who is going to treat me like a dirty little secret."

He sputtered again. She was putting words into

his mouth, except that she was right. Silently, he watched as she climbed the steps back to the house.

And then she was gone, and he had no choice but to get into his car and go.

CHAPTER NINE

Now

BOSTON LOOKED NOTHING like Los Angeles, and Ford loved it.

The drive through the familiar streets, the New England architecture and the leafy greenery soothed his soul. He'd lived in California for two and a half years, and he'd enjoyed the sparkle of it all, the bright lights and eclectic people and towering palms.

But Massachusetts was home.

Working his black SUV through traffic to the South End, he made his way to his new home—a midsize two-story on a large lot. It was a far cry from the waterfront condo he'd once owned on the harbor, or the minimansion he'd inhabited in Los Angeles.

He was happier to be moving in here than he'd been in either of those other places.

For years he'd worked feverishly, building his hotel chain into a global dynasty. He'd been engaged to a woman who suited his life. He'd had everything he'd ever wanted.

He'd been greedy. And he'd lost it all.

A smile quirked the corners of his lips as he turned onto the run-down street. There, the Sold sign still on the lawn, was his new home.

He hadn't lost quite everything.

Slinging his laptop bag over his shoulder, Ford parked the Escape in the driveway and wrenched open the manual garage door, wincing at the screeching sound. He couldn't imagine wrestling with the thing in the middle of winter, so he'd have to look into installing an automatic one. Other than that, he didn't intend to add many other luxuries to the place. In truth, he could have afforded something in a nicer neighborhood. When the German hotel chain he'd partnered with—had trusted—had done a hostile takeover of his company, he'd still had a cushion in the bank. To many people in this neighborhood, it was probably even a small fortune.

To him, it was money to start over. To invest in something fresh. He didn't want to waste any of it on his personal life when it could be used for an investment opportunity.

He didn't know what that opportunity would be yet, but he'd know it when he saw it. He'd built his fortune the first time around by trusting his gut. He could do it again.

The front door creaked as he unlocked it and

pushed it open. The smell of dust greeted him, and he could see the specks of it dancing in the white light of early afternoon.

He certainly hadn't splurged on any luxuries here. The flooring was a mix of worn linoleum and shag carpet straight from the '70s. He'd purchased the place furnished, and the olive-green couch had been shredded by cat claws.

The beige paint was peeling from the plaster walls. Peyton would have hated it.

As he set his laptop bag down in the front entryway, Ford noted that thinking of his former fiancée didn't bring up anything more than a mild bittersweet sensation.

When he'd left Boston for California, he'd been… well, he'd been shaken by what had happened with Beth Marchande. The things she'd pulled from his very core and insisted that he acknowledge.

He'd thrown himself into work, searching for what he thought he wanted. He'd met Peyton Channing at the launch of his Beverly Hills location, and he and the sleek brunette socialite had hit it off.

They had fun together. They were friends. And the sex between them was…nice.

Still, when he'd lost his fortune, she hadn't known quite what to do. She had money of her own—she wasn't a gold digger—but something between them had shifted.

She no longer saw him as her equal. And he—

well, he knew that he'd never really shown her who he was. They'd parted on good enough terms that he knew while he'd loved her, he'd never been *in* love with her.

Wading through the dregs of his life had been an eye-opener. He'd done everything he'd thought he was supposed to do, and look where it had landed him.

An international empire and a sweet vanilla woman hadn't fulfilled him. Moving home, searching for a new business that excited him, and acknowledging who he truly was—*that* was what got his blood pumping now.

Heading to the garage, Ford treated himself to a quick peek inside. There she was, his baby—his now fifteen-year-old Porsche Turbo. He really should sell her, add the money to his investment capital, but he couldn't.

The car was a symbol. He loved it, and it meant something to him, so it was a reminder to be present, to actually live his life instead of getting caught in the trappings of what he thought he should do.

Heading to the kitchen, he washed his hands and splashed water over his face. It smelled faintly of rust, and for some reason that made him grin.

This was his new life, and he couldn't wait to live it.

Mamesie's ancient Honda Civic turned over when Beth put the key in the ignition. She grinned as the old engine rumbled to life, a senior citizen protesting being coaxed from its nap.

The car hadn't wanted to start this morning, so she'd slotted it into her day of appointments, after an ancient pickup that belonged to a friend and a young family's minivan.

The routine felt good. She liked having a structure to her day, enjoyed seeing tangible results from her actions.

It gave her a purpose, something to cling to when she thought that she might fall apart.

"Hey, baby girl." Pushing through the door from the house, Jo shoved her hands into her pockets and whistled a few notes. "How are you feeling? You've been at that for a while."

Beth bit back a sharp retort. She loved all of her sisters, but she and Jo had always had a special bond. That meant her older sister worried about her, though, and fussed without meaning to.

She both appreciated it and resented it. Her sister meant well, but sometimes it was hard enough for Beth to get through the day without being bogged down with worry. Someone else fussing over her just made it worse.

Shaking it off, she climbed from behind the wheel of her mother's sedan. "I'm fine. Mamesie's baby is back up and running. I'm about to break for lunch."

"I was hoping you'd say that." Jo grinned and

hiked up her skinny jeans. "I'm starving. Let's go to the Tearoom and grab some lunch."

"With what money?" Beth felt the familiar guilt as she stripped off her coveralls and headed for the industrial sink to scrub her hands with mechanic's orange-peel scrub. They'd floated along just below the line of comfortable income after her father died, but Beth's illness had sunk them. They'd be paying off her medical bills for years, and it was going to take a miracle to keep their home in the meantime.

"I don't want to see that look on your face, baby girl." Stomping down the steps in her battered Doc Martens, Jo closed the space between them and crossed her arms over her chest. "I don't know how we can make this sink in. We're a family. We handle things together."

Beth pinched her lips together as she reached for a pair of worn jeans to pull on over her spandex shorts. She didn't want to have this argument again.

Especially since she knew Jo was right.

Instead, she tugged the elastic from the bottom of her braid, letting the waves shake free. Turning to her sister, she arched an eyebrow. "Yeah, yeah. Still. Where did you come up with the cash? Shouldn't you give it to Mamesie?"

"I scored a ghostwriting gig that paid up front." Jo scowled at her. "And of course I gave it to Mamesie. But I set aside twenty bucks to celebrate.

And I choose to celebrate with you, so stop being crabby and let's go."

She was being crabby. She'd woken up in a mood that day and it had been hard to shake. She made a deliberate choice to start the conversation over and scurried to catch up with her sister's quick gait as Jo strode out of the garage and started down the street.

"Congrats on the ghostwriting gig." She nudged her sister with her hip, and Jo nudged her back, letting her know that everything between them was fine. "What's it for?"

Her sister grinned wickedly, her amber eyes sparking with amusement. "An erotic romance."

"No way." Beth choked out a surprised laugh. "Don't you usually get contracts for sci-fi?"

"I was getting bored of writing about blonde aliens with three boobs who want nothing more than to worship the human male who stumbled across them." Jo shrugged, her lips twisting sarcastically. "Figured I'd open up the parameters of what I was willing to do. Turns out there are a ton of these erotic romance authors who want to release a book every month but just can't write that fast. Enter Jo."

"Or Jo gets entered." Beth laughed when her sister snorted. "Seriously. How does this work. Do you get an outline like with the sci-fi? Are you going to… hmm, draw on personal experience?"

"Wouldn't you like to know, perv." Gesturing to the strip mall that was their destination, Jo sniffed at the air. "Hurry up. I'm dying for an order of pierogies."

Beth followed her sister into the Tearoom. Not much to look at, the café was an odd but delicious mix of Jewish deli and Ukrainian cuisine.

Her sister ordered a pierogi platter, and Beth's mouth watered as the cafeteria-style setup served a paper plate loaded with the potato-and-cheese-filled dough crescents, topped with fried onions, bacon and an artery-clogging scoop of sour cream.

She hesitated, tempted to get the same. Instead she ordered a spinach salad with dressing on the side.

She didn't particularly like spinach or salad, and she certainly wasn't trying to lose weight. But with her new lease on life, she'd decided to try to treat her body properly. And that meant chewing on chopped spinach and boiled eggs while Jo inhaled deep-fried mashed potatoes wrapped in dough.

Swallowing a particularly fibrous chunk of the spinach, she reached for her water, looking across the tiny eat-in area, into which were crammed eight small tables for two.

The water caught in her throat when she looked right into the face of Ford Lassiter.

"Holy shit." She dropped her fork. Jo swallowed a massive mouthful and swiveled in her seat to see what Beth was staring at. "What?"

"Don't do that!" To get her attention she stole her

sister's fork, and Jo growled. "Simmer down. Just... stop looking."

"Well, what are you looking at?" Jo stole her fork back, her body still half turned in the seat. "The Jolly Green Giant? George Washington? Niall Horan?"

"Remember that suit I had a thing with a few years ago?" Beth reached for her bottle of water, since her throat was suddenly dry. "The one who came to lunch?"

"Uh-huh." Jo cranked her head around again as Beth sighed with exasperation. "What was his name? Felix?"

"Ford." His head snapped up, and she realized that she'd spoken far too loudly. She smiled tentatively as storm-brown eyes focused in on her.

Ford Lassiter. Jesus, talk about a blast from the past. Unconsciously, she smoothed a hand over the kinky waves left by her braid. Did she have spinach in her teeth? She'd been under the hood of Mamesie's car for the last hour. What did she look like?

His brow furrowed, as though he was trying to place her. Her heart sank, and heated irritation surged in an attempt to burn away the disappointment.

Of course he didn't recognize her. They'd fucked twice, and it had been five years since.

She'd never forgotten him.

As she sat frozen, the puzzlement on his face

quickly morphed into pleasure. He grinned and set down his sandwich.

"Beth?" Standing, he approached their table with an open expression, which both delighted and surprised her. "Wow. It's so good to see you."

He held out his arms for a hug, and after a heartbeat of indecision, she rose to welcome the embrace. Over the years she'd thought about this, about what might happen if she ever ran into Ford again. If he'd pretend he didn't know her. If he'd be embarrassed to admit their past to the fancy fiancée that was plastered all over the newspapers.

She'd never imagined that he'd be so openly delighted to see her. Warmth suffused her, and when she stepped into his arms for the hug, the heat cranked up to a roaring flame as her body pressed against his own.

He ran a hand down the length of her hair lightly, then pulled back. The spark in his eye told her that he felt it, too, that same attraction between them. That he still enjoyed the buzz of their chemistry.

She reminded herself that he was engaged.

"I'm sorry I didn't recognize you." He took a step back, but she could still feel the heat from his body. "You've changed your hair."

"Oh." Her hand went to the wild waves again. The length was much the same as it had been five years ago, but prescriptions had thinned it out in the meantime. It was now wavier, a bit wilder. And gone were the days of bright blues and purples and pink—she now settled for a cherry-red henna rinse on her natural light brown. No unnecessary chemicals for her. "Well, it's been a long time. And men are kind of stupid about hair."

He laughed, and she liked the sound. She smiled in return, and when their stares met she felt another little jolt.

Basic chemistry. It was there or it wasn't, and apparently the years hadn't dimmed the potent punch of attraction between them.

"We are pretty stupid about stuff like that." He looked down at her with a face that was still ridiculously gorgeous, and she felt a pulse of adrenaline. "But seriously. It's so great to run into you."

"I'm going to let you two catch up." Jo stood abruptly, gathering up her empty plate and soda can. She waggled her eyebrows suggestively at Beth, who couldn't help grin in reply. "Nice to see you again, Felix."

Ford didn't correct her—he seemed to be too focused on Beth. Gesturing to her half-eaten salad, he cocked his head back to his own table. "May I join you? We can catch up?"

"Yes." Beth exhaled a breath that she hadn't known she was holding. The man still made her a little light-headed. "That would be great."

Ford grabbed his sandwich and soda. Beth stared

at the bright red can, remembering how she'd once seduced him by stealing his Coke for a sip.

"You're in California now, right?" She blurted the words out as a distraction for herself, because she could almost taste the sugar on her tongue. "Are you just back for a visit?"

"Nope." Ford settled into his new seat but didn't dig back into his sandwich. "I've moved back."

A shot of adrenaline surged through Beth. "Did your fiancée move with you?"

Ford took a quick sip of his drink, looking at the can as he set it back down. Beth knew that he was thinking about the exact same thing that she was when his eyes darkened.

"No more fiancée." He swallowed, and she followed the motion of the muscles in his throat. "I'm back for good."

CHAPTER TEN

WHAT THE HELL was Beth Marchande doing back in Boston's South End?

The engine grease smeared on her right cheekbone was the obvious answer—she was working at her garage. But why?

After they'd parted ways, she'd found success with her music. He hadn't followed too closely because it wasn't his kind of thing, but he knew that she'd released a few albums of her original songs. She'd gotten some airplay.

He didn't know what had happened to her after she'd faded from the limelight. In truth, he hadn't wanted to look too closely, because it had been a reminder of what an asshole he'd been to her. But here she was, sitting across from him as he ate his first meal back in the city.

He watched as she picked at her salad. She looked good—great, even. She'd lost a bit of weight since he'd seen her last that she could stand to put back on, but her body was still sexy as hell. She was wearing ripped jeans and a simple black tank top, which showed the arm ink that had fascinated him before, and maybe a few new tattoos.

He tried not to look, but he couldn't help a quick peek at the gorgeous cleavage peeking out of her top. He wondered if she still had that mouthwatering silver bar through her nipple.

God, he hoped so.

"You look good, Beth." She looked up quickly. There was a bit of reserve around her that hadn't been there before, but it didn't hide the interest in her gaze. The chemistry between them was still there, and it was intense.

He really wanted to pursue it. He was free. Was she?

"I have a meeting in twenty minutes. I should get going." He didn't miss the flicker of disappointment in her eyes.

"I should get back to work, too." Smiling genuinely, she stood, packing up the remains of her meal. "It's been good to see you, Ford. Really."

"Wait." He caught her wrist as she turned away. His thumb rubbed once, gently, over the thin skin at the inside of her wrist, and her pulse jumped beneath his touch. She turned back, looking at him with a question in her eyes. "Are you free tonight?"

Heat slowly encased her, like warm oil poured on her skin at a massage. He wasn't asking because he wanted to meet up for an evening of pleasant drinks and chitchat.

He still wanted her. Wanted her again. Whatever the semantics were, it both turned her on and threw her off her game.

She'd never forgotten that night with Ford, not even when her life had fallen apart. Hell, sometimes she pulled the memory out as her own personal porn, remembering the way those bossy hands had felt all over her body.

She also remembered the hurt and confusion she'd pushed through after their encounter. The way her confidence had been shaken because he'd so vehemently denied that he wanted her and what she had to offer, even though she'd known even then that it was his issue, not hers. Was it wise to go there again?

Did she care? The potential for something good had been there. Something hot. It was here again now.

"Why are you in Boston?" The last she'd heard of him had been splashed across a glossy tabloid in the supermarket checkout. It had announced his merger with a massive German corporation and also his engagement to Peyton Channing, the more reserved little sister of notorious party-girl socialite India Channing. "You've really moved back? Why did you leave LA?"

"I take it you don't read the tabloids?"

She furrowed her brow. "Um, why?"

"Never mind." He barked out a laugh. "Anyway, it was front-page news for a while. I partnered with a German conglomerate to expand my hotel chain and was reckless with how much control I gave them. They booted me out. Lassiter Deluxe Hotels is no longer mine."

"Oh my God." Acting on instinct, Beth reached across the table to take his hands in hers with sympathy. "I'm so sorry."

"Don't be." To her surprise, he grinned at her. "It was the best thing that ever happened to me. I was forced to reexamine my entire life. What I found was that I didn't much like it."

"What wasn't to like?" Her voice was skeptical. "Boatloads of cash. A-list invites. Gorgeous woman wearing your ring."

"Does that sound like paradise to you?"

"Hell, no." She shuddered. "Well, maybe the cash."

"I still have some of that." He smirked at her expression. "Enough that I can take a step back and think about what I do want."

"And what is that?" She heard the rasp in her own voice, knew it was because he was winding her up. "What does Ford Lassiter want from life?"

"I want to invest the money I have left in a new business. Something that excites me." His wraith-like eyes studied her face. "And then there's the second part."

"Which is?"

"I don't want to pretend to be someone I'm not anymore." Catching her hand again, he kept his gaze on her face as he stroked his thumb over her palm. She couldn't hold back the small shudder at the sensuous touch. "I've had a lot of time to come to terms with who I am. With what I want."

"And what do you want?" She ran the tip of her tongue over her lips. Her pulse picked up the pace.

"Can't give away everything right off." Releasing her, he picked up his soda and took a sip, grinning down at her.

"Tease."

"You have no idea." The air between them pulsed with promise. She realized that she was wet, just from their conversation.

"Can I take you for dinner tonight?" Dinner, she knew, would be more than that. A whole delicious course more.

He wanted her. She wanted him. Her body was on fire, and it infused her with a hint of the sass that had once come so easily to her.

He wanted her back? She wasn't going to make it a cakewalk for him.

"There's a place a few blocks over. Mamacita's." She sat back in her chair. "Ever heard of it?"

"Nope." His expression was amused. "But I have the miracle of GPS. What time?"

"Seven." She was pleased with herself. If he

wanted to do this, he was going to have to sit through dinner at a place of her choosing. One that she guessed was a few thousand times more of a dive than anything he'd ever set foot in before. "Don't be late."

Tugging at the hem of her tank top, she watched as his gaze flickered down to her chest. She'd noticed his herculean effort to be polite earlier, but now she deliberately pulled the fabric snug, guessing that he was searching for the bump of her piercing.

She could tell the instant he found it, because he hissed out a breath. His gaze returned to her face, and he grinned at her.

"I have no intention of disappointing you like that."

Oh, yeah.

Leaning across the table, she picked up his can of Coke and slowly, deliberately took a sip.

It was answer enough.

CHAPTER ELEVEN

BETH LOOKED GOOD, and she knew it.

With one final, satisfied look at her reflection, she exited the bathroom that she shared with Meg—she was closer with Jo, but Meg and Amy were both bathroom hogs, so they'd split the difference. She'd made sure to tell her eldest sister that she needed the space for at least an hour this evening, and to Meg's credit, she hadn't knocked even once.

Still, Beth braced herself as she followed the sound of her sisters' voices to the kitchen. What would they think about this, her first date in…well. She hadn't been counting, but it was at least a year and a half. Since before she'd gotten sick.

Shoving aside her nerves, she entered the kitchen. Meg, Jo and Amy were seated around the kitchen island, and from the looks of it, Amy was kicking the older two's asses at Crazy Eight Countdown.

They all fell silent as Beth entered, and she winced. Here it came—the worries, the *gentle* questions. The smothering.

Two years ago, she would have flipped them the bird and told them where to go. Now, though? Now there was guilt. The feeling that she had to listen them all, had to take their fears on as her own because she owed them all so much.

Her illness had essentially tied them all to this house. Forever. How could she not feel guilty?

Her defenses started to rise as the other three stared at her. She got ready for the onslaught of concern.

It didn't come. Instead, the three women she was closest to in the world broke into applause.

"I knew I looked good, but I didn't know I looked that good." She grinned as she did a little spin. She wouldn't admit, even here, how long she'd spent deciding what to wear. In the end she'd settled on a little sundress that she'd picked up from her favorite thrift store a couple of months ago and hadn't yet worn. The skirt was short and flared, flirty with its multicolored paisley print. The top had thick straps, dipping into a low vee in both the front and the back.

The material was silky and thin. She'd chosen it both because it made her feel sexy, and because she knew that the thinness of the material would have Ford thinking about her nipple piercing all night.

She finished the look off with tan booties, a chunky white cardigan and just a bit of polish to her hair and nails. She'd pulled on a pair of the little spandex shorts she wore under her coveralls since the skirt was so short, but she'd left off the bra.

She felt damn good.

"You look good, baby girl." Jo looked up from her bowl of cold cereal to give her a thumbs-up while Amy continued to clap her hands with glee.

Meg squinted at her and fake frowned. "That's my eye shadow. But it looks so good, I won't yell."

"You guys are…excited for me?" This was strange. She wasn't quite sure what to make of it.

"Beth, it's been so long. *So* long. It's about time you got back out there." Amy stood up and tucked one of Beth's waves behind her ear.

"I know we all get a little overprotective." Meg and Amy arched eyebrows at Jo as she spoke, and she scowled in response. "Okay, *I* get a little overprotective."

"You think?" Amy muttered. Meg swatted her arm.

"We—*collectively*—" Jo glared at the other two "—have been waiting for this. You were given your life back. You need to live it."

Her sister's voice cracked on the last couple of words, and Beth's heart both swelled and broke at the same time. Wordlessly, she crossed the kitchen to her sister and wrapped her in a big hug. Meg and Amy followed, and within a minute they were all tearing up and laughing at the same time.

"Come on," Meg ordered, shooing the other two away. "I'll drive you."

"I can walk." Though when she looked down at her booties, she wasn't at all sure that she could.

"Let me be the big sister." Meg nudged her toward the back door. "Go."

Enjoying the freshness of the crisp air outside, Beth hauled herself up into Meg's van. Not quite Ford's Turbo, she thought wryly as she buckled herself in, but it would do.

"Have fun." Meg smiled at her when they pulled up in front of Mamacita's. Beth smirked, about to tell her just how much fun she intended to have, but the seriousness of Meg's expression made her stop. "I'm serious, Beth. You deserve this."

Reaching into her bag, she pulled out a small cardboard box and pressed it into Beth's hand.

"Ribbed for her pleasure." She snorted out a laugh. "Always looking out for me."

"Damn straight." Meg stepped on the gas, causing the van to roar and everyone within a half-block radius to stare. "There. Now you can make an entrance. Go!"

"Going!" Beth was still laughing when she entered the restaurant. It was small, dingy and packed with blue-collar types, but Mamacita herself made the best Mexican food on the South End.

The small size made it easy to spot Ford. Hell, she would have zeroed right in on him even if the place had been huge. Part of it was that she seemed to be connected to him with an invisible string whenever he was here, and part of it was that even in his jeans and plain black T-shirt, he would never blend in with the rough crowd.

He moved like a man who got what he wanted, when he wanted it. And as she moved through the room, he was the only one she could see.

"Sorry I'm late." Through the crowd, she slid into the booth across from him. His appreciative stare made the extra effort she'd put into her appearance worth it.

"I'd say you were worth the wait." He grinned at her. "I ordered you a margarita. I figured that's what you'd want here."

"What if I don't want what you have to offer?" Her voice was teasing, but she needed something to ease the tension before she combusted.

"You want it." The grin slipped from his face, replaced with pure heat. "You wouldn't have made the choice to come here otherwise."

"Touché," she conceded, leaning back in her seat. "However, in all fairness, I don't drink. Not anymore."

He cocked his head slightly, and she knew he was wondering why, but he didn't ask. Instead he signaled the waitress and ordered two glasses of Coke.

Beth didn't drink soda anymore, either, the sip of Ford's she'd had earlier not counting in her books.

But tonight was a celebration of starts—a new beginning—so she decided to just go with it.

She expected him to cut straight to the heart of the matter—that they still wanted to be in each other's beds. To seduce her toward what she already knew they would be doing after they left here.

Instead, after they ordered, he led her into conversation. Date-type conversation. Bemused, she let him.

"So you really don't know what kind of business you're going to start up this time?" Her tortilla soup arrived, and she dipped her head to fan a breath over the fragrant steam. "And…wow. You seem so okay with being forced out of your own business. Are you really? Last time I saw you, you were all *my work is my life*."

She grinned sheepishly when he winced. "Sorry. Foot in mouth. Am I poking at a sore subject?"

"No." He spooned steak, grilled peppers and cotija cheese into a tortilla to make one of the fajitas that he'd ordered. She found that she liked watching his hands. "The wince was because of what I sounded like back then. All work, no play makes Ford a dull boy."

"I wouldn't say there was *no* play."

Beneath the table, his knees brushed against hers. She held her breath, waiting—hoping—for him to place a hand on her bare knee. He caught her expression and, reaching under the table, grazed his hand lightly over the sensitive skin beside her kneecap.

Who knew that the knee could be an erogenous zone?

"Don't get me wrong. I raged for a while. Drank my way through half the bars in Los Angeles. Shoved money I no longer had at my lawyers to find a loophole." Reaching for his Coke, he took a sip and shrugged. "At the end of the day, it truly was out of my hands. I'd made some mistakes and had to live with the consequences. And after I finished cursing the world, I realized how much happier I was. I started following that path, and here I am."

"That's admirable." She wished she'd reached the same level of peace.

One day at a time.

"And what about you?" He took a bite of his fajita. "You were famous for a while there. I'm afraid I couldn't name one of your songs, but I know you were making some headway. How come you landed back here?"

Beth felt her smile freeze. She reached for her drink to cover it, sipping until she felt calm again. Getting sick certainly wasn't anything to be ashamed of. But everyone she'd known before getting sick looked at her just a little differently now.

Ford saw her as a woman—a healthy, sexual woman. She didn't want that to change, at least not tonight, so she shook her head to gloss over it. "I had some health problems. Once I stopped to take care of them, I realized that I didn't really miss it."

"Didn't miss touring? Or didn't miss music?" He fastened his gaze on her face. "I remember hearing you play. Watching you. Your whole body got into it."

"I didn't miss touring. Music is part of me. I still play." She poked her fork into her salad. "Now I just upload my songs to YouTube instead of playing them live. I'm happier this way."

It wasn't a lie. Still, she didn't add that touring would never be a good decision for her again. The constant travel and stress was hard on the body, and though she'd been healthy for a year now, she knew that could change in the blink of an eye.

She could tell that he knew there was something more, that he wanted to push, and she was grateful when he didn't.

"What about your sisters? Amy was a tattoo artist, right?"

"Yes. She still is. Meg works for a catering company, and Jo ghostwrites. Books, magazines, whatever comes her way."

"And you all still live at home?"

"We do." She sensed his curiosity. It wasn't unfounded—four grown women still living with their mother was, well, weird. "It works for us. It's our family home, and it's an old house. It eats up a lot of cash in upkeep, but we love it. If one of us moved out, though, the others wouldn't be able to afford it anymore. They'd have to sell. So we stay."

She had no idea what they'd do if any of her sisters got married. The husband to be might protest at moving into a house full of women.

"We get along well," she offered. Still, she saw the question on his face, and she guessed that he wanted to ask what had happened to the money she'd made on her albums and her touring.

Telling him it had all barely made a dent in her hospital bills was a story for another time.

He didn't press. Instead, they ate in comfortable silence for a few minutes. She enjoyed having the time to just watch him. He looked a little older, but that leonine power was still there, and this time it was more potent.

He was more confident in who he was. And it was freaking hot.

As they finished their meal and Ford paid the bill, she felt a clutch of excitement in her stomach. After lunch today, she'd gone back to her shop and mechanically worked her way through her afternoon's jobs. With busy hands, she'd had a lot of time to think about this.

Five years ago, they'd been careless with one another. With a second chance, she wondered if they were ready now.

She couldn't wait to find out.

"After you." He placed his hand at the small of

her back to guide her from the restaurant—which, she was forced to concede, he hadn't blinked an eye at. His fingers were on skin bared by the deep vee of the back of her dress, and her senses hummed from the contact.

Following him outside, she stopped short when she saw the Turbo parked at the curb.

"Risky business, driving that thing in this neighborhood." Reaching out, she ran a hand over the sleek silver finish. Behind her Ford growled low in his throat, and she looked back over her shoulder to see heat painted over his features.

"I thought it was worth it," he said, closing the thin ribbon of space between them. His chest brushed her partially bare back, and she shivered. "I have some really good memories of this car. And you."

"I remember." As if she could forget. She touched herself to that memory more often than she cared to admit, the feeling of being trapped between the cool metal and Ford's hard thrusts a permanent part of her dreams.

One of his hands settled on her waist as he reached around her to open the passenger-side door. Without meaning to, she pressed back against him, and for a moment they just stayed like that, pressed together, absorbing each other's heat.

Hand still on her waist, he urged her to turn around. She gasped when he trapped her against the car with his lean hips, but he did nothing more than open her door for her.

"My place is close." His voice was raw with need, and she thrilled to it.

"Drive fast."

CHAPTER TWELVE

He drove as fast as he dared. Beside him in the car Beth was quiet, but he felt so much intensity, so much need, that there was no way she didn't feel it, too.

Pulling into his driveway, he contemplated getting out to wrench open that damn garage door so he could park the Turbo inside.

It would take too long, time that could be spent with his hands on Beth's soft skin. He'd risk it.

"Welcome to my palace." He held out his hand to help her from the low-slung vehicle. When she swung herself out, he caught a glimpse of the little black spandex boy shorts she was wearing.

Fuck.

He remembered those little shorts. He wanted to have those little shorts in his teeth.

"It's a dump," he warned her as he opened the creaky front door. She laughed, brushing his comment aside.

"My bedroom threatens to turn into a swimming

pool every time it rains. I wouldn't be worried about impressing me."

He shut the door behind them, and the only reason he didn't press her right up against it was because she'd kicked off her shoes and padded forward into his living room.

"Not too shabby, Ford." Bending to flick on a lamp, she treated him to another view of the shorts, this time hugging the sweet, heart-shaped ass from his fantasies. His cock had been at half-mast since he'd pressed her against the car back at the restaurant, and now all the blood in his head rushed to his swollen shaft.

"No need to try to impress me, either. The place is a wreck." Kicking off his own shoes, he followed her into the living room. His cock was straining at the zipper of his fly, but he liked the ache. The anticipation.

"Au contraire, my friend." Beth finished circling the room, stopping in front of a chair upholstered in a geometric print. She pointed to it. "This is a vintage Italian armchair. Midcentury. You could sell it for a few thousand dollars."

"That thing?" He cocked his head. He didn't see it.

"Yes, this thing." Sinking into it, she settled back with a happy sigh. "Don't listen to him. I know what a beauty you are."

"The beauty isn't the chair." And it wasn't. Even against the hideous print, she was stunning. The lamp cast a soft glow over her features, the reddish tint of her hair. He liked that she'd kept a natural look for tonight. As natural as a woman with tattoos sleeving her arms could look.

Opening her eyes, she peered up at him. He stepped farther into the room, standing in front of her. Bending, he placed his hands on her knees, then slowly urged his hands up, up beneath the silky fabric of her dress. He stopped midthigh, and her muscles tensed beneath his hands as he dipped his head to kiss her.

"Mmm." She sighed softly into his mouth, reaching up to work her hands through his hair. "Still got some moves, Sir Lassiter."

Sir Lassiter. He'd dreamed of hearing that from her lips for years. Hearing it again now was a punch of lust straight to the gut.

He wanted her. The need had only gotten better with time, and he wanted to drink her up.

"I could probably be persuaded to like this chair." Easing back, he settled his weight on an ottoman that sat across from it.

"Oh?" She smirked. "Do tell."

"What would you say if I told you to get naked and get back in it?" He noted her quick shudder of excitement.

"I'd wonder why you were asking instead of telling." Her eyes shot blue sparks, and he groaned.

She was challenging him. Asking if he really was

ready to accept everything he'd wanted before but denied them both.

Leaning forward, he settled his elbows on his knees, watching her. He could never get enough of watching her.

"Get naked." His words weren't a question. "I want to watch."

She said nothing, simply pushed up out of the chair. As she turned, his stare feasted on the swirls of colorful ink on her back as she lifted the hem of her dress.

She tugged it up and over her head, then cast it to the floor. She was still facing away, but he was transfixed by her tattoo.

"This is new." He stretched his arm out to drag a single finger down her spine. The ink started at the nape of her neck, lines of music notes that tapered with the shape of her body, ending with a single note at the base of her spine. "It's fucking gorgeous."

"It's the score to one of my songs." She wiggled impatiently, drawing his attention to her ass. Pulling the ottoman closer, he cupped the plump cheeks in his hands, his thumbs grazing the insides of her thighs.

"Fuck," she hissed when he traced just the outside of her lower lips through the thin fabric of her shorts. "You're still good at that."

"I'm better." He repeated the move, enjoying the tremble in her thighs. Moisture dampened the tips of his fingers, and he inhaled the musky, salty scent. "Now turn the fuck around. You know what I want to see and you're hiding it."

She laughed breathlessly as she turned, too slowly for his liking. When she again faced him, her hands were covering her breasts.

"You're a brat." Placing his hands on her hips, he tugged her into the vee of his thighs. That close, he could feel the heat of her skin, and he felt wetness leak from the head of his cock. "I want to see those fucking amazing tits of yours. Show me."

Gaze glued to his, she slowly, deliberately dropped her hands. Her breasts bounced as they were freed, the jiggling of the plump flesh sending a surge of something almost painful through him.

Her right nipple was still pierced. But now, instead of the silver bar, the rosy tip was decorated with a delicate gold hoop.

"Fuck me." The words tore out of him, and then his hands were at her waist, tugging her to him. She gasped when his mouth closed over her nipple. He caught the ring in his teeth and tugged, just a bit, and she wobbled, her hands landing on his chest.

Sucking hard, laving the tip of her breast with his tongue, he urged her down until she straddled his lap. This brought her damp cleft into direct contact with his rock-solid shaft, and he thrust against her instinctively.

She ground down on him when he took her neglected nipple in his fingers, rolling and tugging until it was as swollen as the one in his mouth. He wanted to keep sucking, teasing, grinding—he wanted it all, but it had been five years. He wanted to make it worth the wait.

He pulled his mouth from her breast with a damp pop. Her nipple was red, engorged, wet from his mouth. Sometime soon he was going to play with those fantastic tits all night long. That was all he would do.

At the end of it he'd have her hold them together so he could fuck them. The image was so arousing he started to shake.

"Stand up." He wasn't even sure he was speaking English by this point. She whimpered at the order, rubbing her pussy over his erection until he saw stars. "Do it."

Chest heaving, and breasts jiggling along with it in a way that made his mouth water, she did. He took a moment to trace his fingers over the flock of birds inked onto her rib cage before pushing the ottoman back a foot.

"Lose the shorts." His hands were damp as he settled them on his knees. They were shaking a little.

What *was* this?

He thought she might argue. Instead she hooked her fingers in the waistband on the spandex. With a sensuous little sway, she pulled them down to midthigh, baring a plump, damp pussy that he'd missed for far too long.

"All the way." She kicked them off, standing in front of him naked. Her hair was loose and wild around her shoulders, the ink on her skin highlighting the curves of her body.

How had he ever thought that a woman like her shouldn't be sexy? She was the hottest fucking thing he'd ever seen.

"Sit down in that chair you love so much." Slowly, he undid the buckle of his belt. She did as he ordered, but her eyes were fastened on his fingers as he popped the button on his jeans.

His cock was escaping the confines of his boxer briefs, pressed up flat against his belly. Lifting his hips, he shoved his jeans and underwear down around his hips, freeing his erection fully.

Her stare was fastened to it.

"Hook your legs over the arms of the chair." She did, the crook of her knees settling on the top edge. She was completely naked, open wide to him, and his pulse stuttered.

"It's been far too long since I got to see you." She hissed in a breath when he fisted his erection in his hand. "I want to look my fill, so this is what we're going to do. You're going to play with those tits while I look, while I think about what I'm going to do to that tight little body of yours. I'm going to jerk off while I do it. But if you try to touch that pretty little pussy of yours, then I'm going to finish myself, and you won't get what you want."

"Jesus, Ford." Her breath was coming in pants. "You got good at this."

"Don't talk." Who was this person speaking with his mouth? He was just saying what he wanted, but man, he was a filthy fucker.

This was who he was, and he was going to embrace it this time around. Why the fuck wouldn't he, when it felt so damn good?

Settling in on the ottoman, he moved his hand up and down his length. He could feel his pulse in his cock, and it jumped when Beth cupped her breasts in her hands and rubbed her thumbs over her nipples.

"Yeah. Like that." He jerked himself faster, felt pleasure tightening at the base of his spine. His gaze bounced between the clever fingers plucking at her nipples and the pink lips that looked so wet and ready for his cock.

He prayed that she could keep her fingers out of it, because he didn't know if he had the strength to follow through on his threat.

One of her hands started to travel south, splaying over the soft curve of her belly. Springing forward, he caught her wrist. She cried out as he hauled her up out of the chair, spinning her so that he could lay her out flat on the ottoman.

"I wanted to go slow this time, but you drive me to distraction, woman." Grabbing his T-shirt at the back of the neck, he tugged it up and off. "I'm going to fuck you now. I'm going to fuck you hard."

"Yes. Now!" She writhed where he'd laid her down. Working her way back until her long hair spilled over one end, she planted her heels on the other edge so that she was still wide-open to him. "I have condoms in my purse. Hurry the fuck up."

"Still bossy, I see." He swatted her hip before pulling his wallet from his pocket. "And I've got it covered."

He tore the condom wrapper open faster than he had when he'd lost his virginity, sheathing himself in the latex. Kneeling in front of her, he tucked two fingers inside her hot sheath to make sure she was ready.

She cried out, bucking against his hand. He ran his thumb over her clit and she ground against him, her pussy leaving dampness where it rubbed against his stomach.

"Get ready," he warned her, lining up the head of his cock with her lower lips.

"Fucking do it already!" She rolled her hips in response, begging him to come inside.

He did. Grabbing her by the hips, he surged inside. She was wet, she was hot, she was heaven on his cock. He pushed as far as he could, grunting when she clawed at his chest.

"I forgot how tight you are." Finding her clit again,

he rubbed small tight circles until he felt her melt around him, letting him in the last inch.

In her to the hilt, he stopped, panting. She was splayed out before him, naked and open, hair damp with sweat, nipple ring glinting in the lamplight, thighs trembling around him.

Something in the area of his heart squeezed. He wanted to panic, but her lips curved into a sexy little smile, and he knew that whatever the hell this was, she felt it, too.

"You feel incredible." Her voice was a whisper, barely audible over their combined panting. She gave a little wiggle that had his eyes rolling back in his head. "*Sir.*"

A sound somewhere between a growl and a groan tore from his throat. Clasping her thighs, he placed one of her bent knees on each of his shoulders. She was fully open to him, unable to do more than grab at his biceps as he started to thrust.

"Yes," she breathed against his shoulder as he rocked up into her. "God, I knew you'd be incredible when you finally let yourself go."

He'd show her letting go. One of her thighs slipped from his shoulder as he increased his pace. His pelvis made a smacking sound every time he seated himself inside her, and droplets of his sweat fell from his forehead to splatter wetly across her breasts.

Beneath him, she shuddered. He could feel her body tightening, straining toward release.

His thrusts became impossibly harder. She braced her foot on the floor with the leg that had slipped from his shoulder, and he tucked the other up close to her breasts, bent at the knee. Grasping either side of the ottoman to support his weight, he found himself almost fully on top of her. Her head fell back, over the edge of the upholstery, and her lips were parted.

Utter surrender. That was what she looked like to him. She had no trouble giving in to what she wanted—she never had. And here, with her, all of those old voices that told him real men didn't want this—didn't want rough sex, didn't want to boss women around—were silenced.

His orgasm was close. He could feel the tide rising. Bracing himself on one elbow, body stretched out over hers, he pulsed once, twice, three times, shuddering through his release. He caught her nipple ring in his teeth as he shook, and her pussy clenched around him like a vise as she came, too.

Beth had convinced herself over the years that the sex she'd had with Ford couldn't possibly have been as good as she remembered. And it wasn't—it was better.

His weight sprawled out over top of her felt decadent. She couldn't help but laugh, and he joined her as he pressed his damp forehead against her breast.

"You just about killed me." He nuzzled against her nipple ring, and even though she'd just come, she felt a tight jolt that shot straight to her core. "Hell of a way to christen the place, though."

She nodded in agreement. As he peeled himself up off her, then helped her to a sitting position, she found her knees were wobbly. She brushed her hair out of her face as she tried to center herself again.

Instead, as Ford hitched on his jeans, then headed to kitchen to grab two bottles of water from the fridge, she found herself staring at him. This—them together again—felt so incredibly surreal that she kept questioning if it was all a dream.

A nagging little voice in her head tried to peck its way through her postcoital bliss. She hadn't been with anyone since she'd gotten sick, because she'd wanted to focus on herself, on staying healthy and enjoying the life she'd been given a second lease on.

Well. She'd learned the hard way that life didn't give a shit about what you'd planned or what you'd wanted.

She wasn't in any position to be thinking far down the road. She wasn't sure that she ever would be. But he was here right now, and this time he wanted the same thing she did—to act on that insane chemistry between them.

Ford returned from the kitchen and pressed a water bottle into her hand. When she smiled at him in thanks and their eyes met, something hot and sweet settled into her veins.

Something good, something real had just happened here. And she wanted to enjoy it for as long as she could.

CHAPTER THIRTEEN

BETH WAS STILL smiling two weeks later as she hovered outside Jo's door. When her sister didn't answer her knock, she shifted the scalding mug of coffee to the other hand and banged on the entrance with her fist.

The door shuddered as it finally flew open, revealing her sister's irritated face. A tuft of black hair stuck out over her ear and she had ink on her nose.

"I come in peace." Beth held her free hand up, palm out. "Thought you could use a caffeine fix, that's all."

"Thanks." Grabbing the mug, Jo took a large gulp, hissing at the heat. She followed it with a more cautious sip. "You didn't make this."

"Nope." Beth didn't drink coffee anymore, but when she had, she'd figured that the stronger, the better. She'd been really good at brewing what her sisters called sludge. "Meg brewed a pot, so I stole you a cup. I think she put cinnamon in it."

"You're a goddess." Jo took another sip, then gestured for Beth to come in. "I just finished this chapter. I'm due for a break."

Beth followed her sister into the room, grimacing as she did. The patchouli scent of the incense that was burning was strong enough to make her eyes water, and it was layered with the burning hint of too many electrical plugs and a staleness that said Jo hadn't left the room for a while. Without asking, she crossed the small room and cranked open the window, letting fresh air circulate.

Jo settled herself cross-legged on her unmade bed. Beth took the thrift-shop chair that was pulled up to the plywood slab and sawhorse that her sister used as a desk. Legal sheets covered in illegible, cramped handwriting covered the desk, and she caught a glimpse of some very naughty words on the screen of the old laptop before it went to sleep.

"The erotic piece?" She cocked her head toward the computer, wishing she'd brought herself some tea.

"You bet." Jo grinned, wrapping her hands around the mug. "I have three bicurious men and one very bad girl on the page right now. Swords are about to fly."

"Sounds titillating." Beth grinned. "Send me a copy when you're done. And give me some warning so I can buy some batteries."

"Don't be greedy. Save the batteries for those of us who aren't getting laid right now." Jo arched an eyebrow at her sister. "How's it going with Felix, anyway?"

"Ford," Beth corrected automatically.

"Well?" Jo sat back, clearly expecting details. Beth opened her mouth to reply but found herself hesitating.

The last two weeks had been, quite simply, amazing. The more than Ford embraced his kink, the better it got for both of them—he fucked her better than she'd ever had it before, and she was pretty sure it was the same for him. And more than that, she actually liked him. When they weren't rolling around naked, they actually had fun together. Despite their obvious differences, they had more in common than she ever would have guessed, from their mutual love of a nice sleek Porsche to the fact that they both enjoyed weird viral YouTube videos.

"The man is good with his hands," she finally admitted, drumming her fingers on her sister's desk. "You're right that I don't need the batteries."

"That's all you have to say about it?" Jo cocked her head. "You've had a smile on your face since you spotted him at the Tearoom. Obviously the sex is good. What gives?"

"Nothing gives." Beth made sure that her expression remained neutral. "We're having fun. I don't need him to propose or anything."

When her sister's toffee-colored gaze narrowed in

on hers, Beth knew she wasn't fooling her. Jo knew her better than anyone else in the world.

But she didn't know everything. She didn't know that sometimes Beth couldn't sleep because of the oppressive guilt that weighed her down until she felt like she couldn't breathe.

Her family was in their current financial situation in because of Beth. For so long now, their lives had revolved around her health. She knew they only cared that she stayed well, not about the money, but knowing that she'd so dramatically changed the dynamic of their family was a cape of stress that she could never shed.

And over all of that was the fact that she could get sick again anytime. Logically, she knew that the guilt she felt was self-destructive, but she couldn't help it.

She was obsessive about monitoring her health so she didn't get sick again because she couldn't handle the thought of being a burden. Ford? The man had lost his empire. The last thing he needed was to be saddled with her, the possibility of more massive hospital bills an albatross around his neck.

They liked each other. They had fun together. They rocked each other's worlds. Why did it have to be more than that?

"You know, you make a point of proving that you can still do everything else you could before you got sick." Jo cast her a sidelong look. "So why would you hold back from someone who makes you feel good? If anyone deserves to be happy, it's you. Even if I find it questionable that you chose a guy named Felix."

Beth rolled her eyes, choosing to focus on that rather than what her sister was trying to say. She held back for a reason. It was her choice.

"I've got to get back to work." Jo stretched. "I need a massive amount of words today in order to get that story in on time."

"Give me your mug. I'll take it downstairs for you." Standing, Beth reached for the empty cup. The light from the window shifted, and the dark purple smudges beneath her sister's eyes became more pronounced.

Narrowing her eyes, she looked around the room. Jo hibernated when she was really into her work, but she usually surfaced at least once a day to shower and track down something to eat. It was Saturday and she hadn't seen Jo since… Thursday?

"Why are you working so hard on the weekend?" Setting the mug back down, she began to prowl around the room. The laundry hamper was overflowing, and the wastebasket was crammed full of empty Pringles cans and Starburst wrappers.

Having made the circle of the room, she stopped in front of her sister. Crossing her arms over her chest, she waited.

"I may have picked up an extra contract. Or two."

Jo lifted her chin defiantly. "I'm just a little stressed. What's your point?"

"You're always really good about not taking on more than you can handle." Jo wasn't telling her something.

Beneath her stare, her sister squirmed, then finally huffed out a breath that sent her wayward tuft of hair dancing. "We have a balloon payment on our mortgage coming up. We're all trying to make a little extra this month."

What? No one had said anything about a big payment to her. Though when she thought of it, just last night Mamesie had enlisted her to help upload listings of her pottery to Etsy, when she normally only did it once a month. Meg had been working a lot of lunchtime functions as well as at night, which she didn't normally do, and Amy hadn't come home from her tattoo shop until eleven the night before.

Jo winced just as Beth put it together. "You didn't tell me on purpose."

The guilt was a fog, gathering thick and fast, so heavy that she couldn't see, couldn't breathe.

They hadn't told her because they didn't want to stress her out. Stress increased the chance of her relapsing.

She knew they didn't want her to relapse because they didn't want her to be sick again. But was there a small part in any of their minds that thought they *literally* couldn't afford for her to get sick again.

"I am not happy with you. With any of you." Beth rarely lost her temper—not the full-force tsunami of it, at any rate—but she could feel her rage bubbling up, about to boil over and scald anyone in its path. "You just finished telling me that I shouldn't let my illness change how I lived my life. That I can do everything I could before. Were you just trying to make me feel better?"

"Simmer down, princess. You know I wasn't." Jo planted her hands on her hips. "You almost died, Beth. Why the fuck can't you just let us take care of you once in a while?"

"Because I don't need to be taken care of!" She had so much to say, but most of it caught in her throat, choking her. She settled for an inarticulate growl before whirling on her heel and storming from the room. She slammed the door hard enough to make it shudder for good measure.

She met Meg coming up the stairs. Her sister wore a white blouse covered in fresh mustard stains and smelling of French fry grease. Now that she was looking for them, she saw that her oldest sister had dark shadows beneath her eyes as well.

"What the hell are you and Jo getting into it about?" Meg tugged the elastic from her tight ponytail, letting the length of stick-straight hair fall free. "I could hear you from the garage."

"How about the fact that my entire family thought I was incapable of contributing to a big payment we have coming up without breaking?" Beth spat the words out. She was pretty sure she'd never been so mad. Felt so betrayed.

Meg bit her lower lip and looked away.

"Yeah, that's what I thought." Beth shook her head with disgust. "I can't deal with any of you right now. I'm going out. Don't wait up."

CHAPTER FOURTEEN

FORD DIDN'T ANSWER his door when she rang the bell. She'd been over enough times in the last two weeks that she felt comfortable heading around the side of the house when she heard the buzz of some kind of power saw from the back.

She stopped dead when she entered the backyard and found her man stripped to the waist despite the chill in the late-September air. Safety goggles were strapped to his head, work gloves were on his hands and a sheen of sweat shone on his hard torso as he ran a two-by-four through a battered power saw.

She'd stormed out of the house knowing that she'd head to Ford's. She hadn't known exactly why, only that he was the one she wanted to help soothe her.

Finding him here looking he'd stepped out of a very dirty dream instantly turned her fury to lust. There were lots of ways to work off a mad, and this was her favorite one.

Unzipping her hoodie, she crossed the yard. She

watched the rock-solid planes of his biceps flex as he set aside the first piece of wood and lifted another.

With every other lover that she'd had, the desire, the wanting had faded a little every time. With Ford? Every time they had sex her need grew thicker, deeper.

Whether it was still just chemistry or if it was because she knew what he could do to her, she didn't care. But she wanted him right now, wanted to use the pleasure he could bring her to edge out the anger, even if just for now.

Closing the space between them, she waited for him to notice her. When he did he grinned, setting aside the piece of wood he was working on and powering down the saw.

"I was just cutting some replacement planks for the deck, but you're much more interesting." Tugging off his gloves, he tossed them to the ground, then drew her in for a kiss. Brushing his lips over hers, he pulled her in slowly, but she was impatient, rising to her toes and fisting her hands in his hair. When they broke apart, she saw the banked fire in his stare and smiled wickedly.

"You look like you're going to eat me alive." He tugged gently on a chunk of her hair, and the nerves in her scalp sparked to life. "Wanna share with the class?"

"I'm angry like I've never been angry before." She bared her teeth when he tugged again. The stiffening of his body against hers made her clarify. "Not with you. But I need to burn it off." Tilting her head back to expose the line of her throat, which she'd learned was a huge turn-on for him, she gasped as he traced his tongue down it. "Interested?"

In answer, he slid his hands down to cup her ass. When he lifted her off her feet, she wrapped her legs around his waist, her arms around his shoulders. Her nails raked over the bare skin of his shoulders.

"I'm pretty sweaty. Want me to shower?" His hands explored the curves of her ass through the thin fabric of her yoga pants, paying particular attention to the cleft that divided her cheeks. She shuddered at the dark promise of his touch.

"Fuck, no." Rolling her hips against his taut stomach, she dipped her head. She ran her tongue over the hard muscle of his shoulder, savoring the taste of salt.

"That's so hot." Striding with her across the deck that he was working on, he propped her against the door frame. Still cradling her ass in one hand, he used the other to cup the breast with the piercing. He growled as he rubbed a thumb over it, making need tighten inside her.

"I think you've got yourself a little fetish there," she teased as she arched into his touch. "Never would have guessed that piercings would turn your crank when you first walked into my garage."

"I have a Beth fetish." Pressing his forehead to hers, he looked into her eyes as he slid his hand inside the camisole she wore under her hoodie. Tugging the thin cotton of her bra beneath her breast, he plucked at the hoop, and she ground her hips into him.

"Now. I want you now." She clawed at his bare chest, knowing but not caring that she was probably leaving welts. "Damn it, Ford. I need this."

"You need what I tell you that you need." He sucked in a breath after he spoke, as if waiting to see her reaction. It did funny things to her insides to see him still finding his footing with what he wanted, who he really was.

And on a whole other level, his words made her so, so hot.

"I told you what I need." The words spilled out of her before she could think them through. Like he had, she paused, holding her breath to see what he thought about the new aspect she'd just added to their game.

They studied each other for a long moment, her bright blue eyes swallowed up by the intensity of his brown ones. There was time for either of them to back out, to make sure that this was what they both wanted.

"You'll get what I decide to give you." With agonizing slowness, Ford cupped his large hand around her throat gently. The spicy scent of cedar drifted to her nose, and she couldn't hold back the shudder.

"Thought so." He smirked. Balancing her with

one hand, he threw the screen door open, carrying her through. The back door led to a small laundry room that had probably been in style when Mamesie was a baby, but when he tugged at her hair again and roughly settled her on the ancient washing machine, she thought she could make herself right at home.

"Bastard." Playing the game, she shoved at his chest. He caught her wrists, twisted them up and over her head, holding them with one large hand. Her chest was thrust forward, and he used his free hand to tug her camisole and her bra below both breasts. Dipping his head, he caught her nipple ring between his teeth and tugged, and she cried out.

"That's what I thought." With a smug smile, he did it again, and she felt the answering pull in her pussy. "Why are you fighting it? You want what I've got, baby."

"Is that the best you can do?" she panted.

His eyes glinted darkly as he reached behind her. Twisting a knob on the washer, he set the machine rumbling beneath her.

"You don't mind if I multitask, do you?" Splaying one hand over her naked breasts, he pressed her down against the vibrating surface. "Since you think you're running things here?"

"Oh, God." Her legs were splayed around his hips, her thinly clothed pussy pressed against the machine, and when he pushed her down the vibration woke up nerves that she hadn't even known she had. She tried to close her legs against the sudden onslaught of sensation, but only succeeded in hugging his hips.

"Still think you know best?" Dipping his head, he nipped at her lower lip, just enough to sting, then released her wrists. Splaying his hand over her belly, he slipped inside the waistband of her yoga pants, heading straight for her cleft and dipping three fingertips inside. "You're fucking soaked. Seems you like what I do just fine."

"Put your cock where your fingers are and maybe you can redeem yourself." A bolt of adrenaline followed her words as she sassed him. This was a game, a hot, filthy game, but the intensity on his face had her fully invested. "That's all I've asked for. Seems like a real man would give it to me."

She gasped when he abruptly slid his fingers from her pussy. Had she gone too far?

She felt the cold kiss of air between her legs as he yanked at her pants, hard. Using fingers still wet with her arousal, he ripped the seam of her pants, under which she wore nothing.

"You'll get it," he promised, releasing her. She cupped her own breasts, lifting them for his gaze as he quickly undid his belt and lowered the zipper of his jeans. "You'll get it when I'm damn well ready to give it to you."

She gasped when pressed a hand against her back, bending her forward so that her cupped breasts were against her knees. When he fisted his cock and slid the head into her cleavage, she thought she just might stroke out.

"Maybe I should just fuck these pretty tits instead of your pussy." He slid the hand from her back up to her hair, running his fingers through the silky strands. "Come all over this sexy little ring and leave you all hot and bothered."

"Do that and I'll just finger myself." He worked his cock a little farther into her cleavage, and she lowered her lips and ran her tongue over it. "You can't stop me."

She gasped when he pulled from between her breasts abruptly, yanking her back up to a sitting position. Pushing her legs so wide that her hips protested, he lined his erection up with the rip in her pants, and ran his head through the folds.

"Keep those clever little fingers of yours out of your pussy," he ordered as he wedged his swollen head against her slick entrance. "Your orgasms belong to me, and I won't have you keeping any of them from me."

"Now. For the love of God, Ford, fuck me now!" She dropped all pretense of the game, body wound so tight she thought that she might shatter. Digging her fingernails into his shoulders until he hissed, she rocked forward, taking him an inch inside her.

"Fuck." He exhaled slowly as she clenched around him. Her breath escaped her on a strangled cry when, with one thrust, he seated himself the rest of the way, stretching her wide-open.

"Yes," she hissed before sinking her teeth into his ear. "More. Now."

He said nothing. Instead, his hands slid to her hips, grabbing them tightly. He pulled her back an inch before slamming them together again, completely controlling her movements.

She wanted more. Bracing her hands on the surface of the washing machine behind her, she leaned back, changing the angle, allowing his solid erection to hit an even deeper spot inside her. Her head fell back, her lips parting as he stroked through her tight flesh.

"I wish you could see yourself right now." He slammed into her again, gaze fixed on the point where they were joined. "You look so dirty. Couldn't even wait to get naked. Demanded my cock and couldn't wait."

"I am dirty," she breathed, looking down the length of her own body. Her breasts bounced and jiggled with every movement, and the view between her legs was obscene, his cock stretching her wide, her pussy leaving him wet. "And you're dirty, too."

"Yeah." He shuddered out a breath, and she could see his excitement visibly rise, all from her words. "You'd better finger that pretty little clit of yours anyway, because I'm close."

"Yes, Sir Lassiter." He moaned, his pace increasing. Bracing herself on one hand, she slid the other over her belly and to the rip between her thighs. Circling the tight knot of flesh, the tips of her fingers brushed his cock as he moved, and they both clenched as need ratcheted higher.

"Come for me, Beth." His thrusts became sloppy, losing the rhythm as his movements turned frantic. She circled her clit quickly, her legs trying to close as her excitement rose.

With his grip on her hips, he pressed her ass down harder on the rumbling washing machine. The vibrations shot through her flesh straight to her pussy, setting off a chain reactions of explosions inside her.

"Ah!" Her hoarse cry echoed off the ceiling of the small room. She clenched around him as he continued to work his way through her swollen flesh, her pleasure a razor-sharp edge that centered entirely on his cock.

He growled and shoved inside her with one fierce, final thrust. She felt the hot pulse of him between her thighs, vaguely registered that she probably shouldn't be feeling that, then decided she didn't care as his movements triggered an aftershock.

Wrapping her arms around his neck, Beth laid her head on his shoulder as she struggled to catch her breath. His chest heaved against hers, heat sealing them together.

"We have a problem." Running a hand down her spine, he looked down into her face cautiously. She nodded, shifting on the machine, wincing as she felt the sticky heat between her thighs.

"I'm on the pill." She swallowed hard. "And I'm clean."

"I am, too." He kept his stare centered on her face, and she felt her nervous pulse begin to slow. It was probably stupid, trusting him so soon.

But it wasn't really that soon, was it? They had history. Plus, she'd been over here so much in the last two weeks, he wouldn't have had any time to fuck another woman. Not that she thought he would.

"So we're good." She ran a hand over her forehead, wiping away the sweat that slicked the skin there. "We probably shouldn't do that again, though."

"I don't know if I can go back to a condom after that." His words were raw and honest. "That was... God, but that was hot, Beth. I lost my mind a little at the end there. I wanted to mark you from the inside out."

"You say the sweetest things." She grinned and he laughed. Her mirth turned to a gasp when he slid his hands up her body, squeezing her breasts before easing out of her.

"I'm serious, though." Reaching for a pile of folded towels that sat on the dryer, he grabbed a facecloth. She was shocked when he rubbed it between her legs, cleaning her up before tossing the used cloth into the sink.

She hadn't expected that. But…it was nice to be taken care of.

"If you're on the pill. And we're both clean." Catching her head in his hands, he slid his palms over her cheeks slowly, stroking the lines of her cheekbones with his thumbs. "I don't want to pressure you. But I'd like to trust each other."

"Fuck, yes." A distant alarm bell rang in the far recesses of her mind, but she ignored it. This was a level of intimacy she hadn't been prepared for.

Right now she wanted it.

"It's going to be even harder to keep my hands off you now." Pressing a kiss to her lips, he twitched his lips in the direction of her clothing. "It probably doesn't bode well for the state of your wardrobe."

"But I feel better." Grinning, she let him help her off the washing machine. "If you find me picking fights with people, you'll know it's so I can come over here and take it out on you after."

"Want to talk about it?" She was startled again when he hooked his fingers in the waistband of her yoga pants and slid them down, helping her out of the ruined clothing. Sorting through another bin of clean laundry, he tossed her a pair of plaid flannel boxer shorts. "I don't have anything else that will fit you. You're going to have to do the walk of shame when you go home."

"There's no shame involved." Her voice was quiet, the words chosen carefully. Ford had come a long way from the man she'd first met, the one who had been terrified of who he was and what he wanted. Still, she saw those hints of uncertainty, of wonder far more often than she wanted, as though he couldn't really believe that this was what she actually wanted.

He met her gaze, then nodded. Message received. Satisfied, she started to strip off her camisole and bra, doing her best to hide her smile when he cocked his head at her questioningly.

"Not that I'm complaining," he said, stare fastened on her breasts as she bared them, "but I don't believe I tore those."

"They're all stretched out, though." Blinking at him innocently, she tossed them aside. "Can't go around in that."

"You're evil." Reaching for yet another piece of laundry, he handed her a pale blue button-down shirt. "There. If you walk around with those fantastic tits out, I'll be inside you again before you can count to three."

"That doesn't exactly give me a reason to get dressed," she pointed out, though she shrugged into the shirt. It was far too big, and she had to roll the cuffs up several times before her hands emerged.

"You can run around topless in a bit. Far be it from me to hold you back." He caught her attention by shoving his own pants down his hips. When they hit the floor, he stepped out of them.

"What are you doing?" She was thoroughly distracted by the sight of his now half-hard cock, which was still hanging out of his boxer briefs. She scowled her disapproval when he picked up a pair of athletic shorts.

"I was working on the house when you showed up and demanded that I let you ride me." He grinned when she rolled her eyes. "I've lost time, so you're going to have to help me make it up."

"Doing what?" He pulled the shorts up around his waist, but before he could tuck himself back in, she reached out and grabbed his waist. "Wait."

Treating herself to the fully lewd view, she tangled their fingers together, then lowered their hands to his still swollen member. Licking her lips, she clasped their twined hands around his length, helping him to tuck himself back into his underwear.

"You're so evil," he gasped when she kept her hand in his pants, their fingers still twisted together. Stare still fixed on the juicy head of his now rapidly hardening cock, she helped him to pump his own length several times, working him back to a full erection.

Then she quickly removed her hand and stepped back, busying herself with tying back her long tangles of hair. She hissed out a breath when, in retaliation, he slid one hand inside her borrowed shirt, tweaking her pierced nipple a handful of times until it was hard with arousal.

"Come on, my little nymphomaniac." He chucked

her under the chin, then pressed a soft kiss to her lips. Her pulse sped.

She was starting to have feelings for him—too many feelings. She was going to have to think long and hard about that tonight.

But for now, she struggled to process what he was saying. When she understood, she thought he was joking.

"Let's go frame some drywall."

CHAPTER FIFTEEN

"MY SISTERS WOULDN'T make me do this."

Ford looked up from where he knelt on the living room floor. He was checking the frame he and Beth had just constructed, making sure all the measurements were correct before they lifted it up for installation.

She made quite a sight. Standing on a short ladder, her arms were above her head as she checked that the top plate they'd installed was secure.

She was still in his boxer shorts and shirt, but she'd refused to button it closed. He had a very nice view of her sexy-as-sin breasts, which he knew was supposed to torment him.

He was enjoying every delicious minute of it.

"You distracted me earlier." His tone sounded like butter wouldn't melt in his mouth. "This is your punishment."

"It's actually kind of nice." She spoke softly just before she climbed back down the ladder, and he wasn't sure that he'd heard her properly.

She met his gaze, and he knew that she'd meant for him to hear. He held his breath, searching for the right thing to say, not wanting to scare her off if she was ready to open up to him.

"Well, you're a mechanic. A musician. You like working with your hands."

"True." Crossing to him, she sank down cross-legged on the carpet and stole his bottle of water. He tried not to read into the intimacy of her action. "But I meant it's nice to be treated like I'm capable of doing something physical. Yesterday Amy caught me carrying a pickup motor, something I've done a million times before. She nearly shouted the house down."

"Is it because you were sick?" He kept his eyes on the pine frame, not wanting to spook her. "Is that why you were angry when you came over today? You had a fight with your family?"

"I had a fight with Jo." She toyed with the cap to the water bottle. A streak of her red-washed hair hung over her left eye, but she didn't bother to brush it back. "Look, you've been to our house. You know we're not exactly rolling in it."

"Hmm." He was noncommittal. He just wanted to keep her talking.

"Anyway. I've told you we all live together so we can afford to keep that house. Apparently we have a big balloon payment coming up, but no one told me. I found out by accident."

She shook the strand of hair out of her face. "They kept it from me because they didn't want to stress me out and make me sick again."

"Beth, what happened to you?" His concern for her trumped worry over her family's financial state. "I wish you'd tell me."

She shook her head vehemently. "It's in the past. I'm fine now. That's all you need to know."

Her refusal to open up stung, he couldn't lie. She'd agreed to no more condoms, trusting him with her body, but she wouldn't share what had happened that had brought that reserve to the woman he'd known.

He could only hope she'd open up in time.

"What made you decide to come back to Boston?" Clearly she wanted to change the subject. Fine. He wouldn't push...for now. "You've told me some. But I'd like to hear more."

Walking on his knees to the next frame, he got out his measuring shape to double-check that it was the size he wanted.

"I wanted to come home." Satisfied with the measurements, he reached out a hand for the bottle of water she still held. Taking it back, he drained it in two swallows.

"When I went to Los Angeles, I was consumed with the idea of what my life should be. My hotels were doing so well, why shouldn't I live in the land of excess? Why shouldn't I spend my time with famous, pretty people?" Tossing the empty bottle aside, he leveled her with a look. "I suspect a shrink might discover that I was trying to build myself up into what I wanted to be because a certain woman with tattoos and a nipple ring had made me take a good hard look at who I really was, which sure as shit wasn't that."

She blushed, something he hadn't seen her do before. "I never meant to make you feel like crap."

"Sure you did." He grinned. "And I needed it. I might never have wound up back here if it wasn't for that, so don't feel bad. In fact, thank you."

She pressed her lips together but said nothing.

"Anyway. When I lost everything, I realized that I didn't even like California. Too hot. Too many people." He shrugged. "When Peyton and I broke up, there was nothing keeping me there anymore. I wanted to come home."

"If she ditched you because you lost your money, she never really loved you." Beth's words were both brutal and true. He barked out a laugh. He didn't need to even probe at his feelings for his former fiancée, because he already knew that he no longer had any.

"She did love me, in just the same way that I loved her." A primitive part of him beat its chest when he watched Beth's eyes narrow. "As friends. She didn't dump me because I'd lost my fortune. Not really. She had plenty of cash of her own. It was that she'd wanted the man she thought I was, not the one who emerged after the dust settled. She wanted someone to go to Hollywood parties with her, to stand by her side as an equal. And she equated money with that equality."

He shrugged. "It was never meant to be."

Beth was silent for a moment, apparently digesting that info. Then she scowled, and he didn't have the heart to tell her that the expression made her look cute. "She still better pray I never meet her. I can't guarantee there won't be a tire iron in my bag."

Surprised laughter exploded out of him; he couldn't help it. Jesus, but she was fantastic. Reaching for her, he tugged her across the short expanse of worn carpet that separated them and planted a firm kiss on her lips.

"What was that for?" She batted at him, but she was grinning.

"Your little violent streak makes me hot." He waggled his eyebrows lewdly. "Next time you go after someone with a tire iron, please let me watch. Please."

She tried to hold back her smile, but the corners of her lips quirked upward. "Yeah, yeah." Settling back into his arms, she sighed.

He held his breath.

"I guess this kind of reminds me of when I stopped touring." She sucked in a deep breath, then slowly exhaled. "You know, getting label attention, getting a record deal for my weird, quirky piano music? That was a one-in-a-million shot. I was so fucking lucky. There were thousands—probably hundreds of thousands—of people who would have done literally anything to be in my place.

"I enjoyed it at first. The attention, the chance to share my music. The money—I was finally able to treat my sisters, Mamesie to a taste of the life that they deserved."

"But?" He was dying to hear the but.

She smiled wanly. "But touring really took its toll. The shows, the press—it was too much. I'm an introvert, you know."

He coughed. She glared.

"You don't have to be shy to be an introvert. I'm not shy, obviously, but being around so many people all the time—it drained me. So when I got sick, at first…at first I was relieved." Casting a sidelong look at him through her lashes, she was clearly waiting for him to judge her. It wasn't going to happen.

"Of course, then shit blew up in my face. I was forced to quit touring. All the money I'd made…well, it was needed for something else." He watched the shadows move across her face, the shutters coming down. She was glossing over what he most wanted to know—what had happened when she was sick—but he had no right to demand that information. Not yet. "But the truth is, that life that I had? Turned out it wasn't really what I wanted after all."

Shifting in his arms, she rose to her knees. Dipping her head to press a kiss to his lips, she smiled up at him with a hint of the shyness that she professed not to have. "So what I'm trying to say is, I get it."

He was a goner.

This woman had been through so much, and yet she was so strong. But even as he thought about that, the shadows of guilt that never quite left him grew darker, clinging to his skin.

She'd glossed over it, but he got the impression that her health still wasn't exactly what it could be.

He was rough with her. Jesus, not two hours ago he'd used her so thoroughly that he'd left the lightest shadows of bruises on her hips. He could see them now, soft violet against her ivory skin.

She wanted it that way. He wanted it that way. But in that moment, hot panic clawed at his throat.

A real man wouldn't bruise his woman. He wouldn't fuck her on top of a washing machine and forget to use a condom.

If he told her the thoughts clouding his mind, she'd call him a coward and accuse him of hiding who he really was.

She'd be right.

Holding on to that, he pulled himself from the mire of his own mind. He and Beth did these things because that was what got them off—got them both off.

He was not his father. He knew his father was into some kinky shit, though he'd always tried to ignore it, but it was the way the older man treated the woman in his life that had left a lasting impression on Ford. It didn't matter if they were wives, girlfriends, mistresses or strippers he'd brought home from his club. In his head, they were there to please him, and the second they didn't, they were gone. No regard for what they wanted or how they felt.

Ford supposed he was lucky he wasn't more fucked-up.

Damn it, he wasn't Bruce. He could be the man he really was—it didn't mean that he didn't treat women well, or care about what they wanted.

Hell, the reason he was able to even think that way was because he wanted to make one specific woman happy.

"I could fall in love with you." Maybe it was endorphins from the sex, maybe it was the vanilla and engine grease scent wafting from Beth's soft hair. He usually had more of a filter, considered big steps like telling someone something like that.

It was true, and he wanted her to know.

In his arms, she froze. He waited, holding his breath, suddenly feeling like he was in the back seat of a limo at prom, pants around his ankles, hoping that Jennifer St. Morrisette would actually let him lose his virginity to her.

Except worse. The waiting now was worse.

Slowly, Beth sat up. Turning to face him, he noted

the sudden rush of rose into her cheeks, the widening of those sapphire-blue eyes.

"Thank you."

CHAPTER SIXTEEN

"EXCUSE ME, MISS. Where can I put my keys? I have an appointment for an oil change."

Beth froze at the sound of Ford's voice. She'd know it anywhere. Slowly, she turned around, eyeing the Turbo that he'd edged up the driveway.

"You don't have an appointment. Chevy Lattner has an appointment." As soon as she spoke, she heard it. Closing her eyes, she pressed a hand to her temple. "Ford, Chevy. Got it. Very clever."

"I wouldn't have had to be sneaky if you weren't avoiding me." Holding up a white plastic bag, he leaned a hip against his car. Her pulse quickened. "I brought dinner."

Why the hell did he have to look so damn good? Especially when she felt like crap? Yeah, she'd been avoiding him. She missed him like hell, but she knew it was the right thing to do.

He'd all but told her that he loved her. That was… bad.

"Ford, maybe we can have dinner next week." She

took a deep breath. "I don't have time right now. If you don't actually have an appointment, then I could use that time to get ahead on the rest of my work."

"Oh, I have an appointment. An oil change takes what, an hour? So I've booked an hour of time at Marchande Motors. If I don't get that hour, I'll be forced to leave a very nasty review on Yelp."

Beth rolled her eyes. He took advantage of her momentary softening to stride forward, close enough that she could feel the heat from his body. "Come on. You'd be eating dinner anyway, right? Eat it with me."

She pinched her lips together, unconvinced.

"I brought taco salad from Mamacita's." He smiled hopefully, and she couldn't help but melt just the tiniest bit.

Damn fool. What did he have to go and fall in love with her for, anyway?

Setting the bag of takeout on the workbench, he placed his index finger under her chin, tilting her face up for a look. She tried to jerk away—in her state of mind, it made her feel too exposed—but he just followed.

"You don't look good," he stated bluntly, making her scowl. "What the hell is going on?"

"Always with the sweet talk." Her words were dry. Jerking away from him, she tugged off her coveralls. She knew he wouldn't go away until she agreed to eat with him.

Tucking a finger into the strap of the tank top that she wore beneath them, he drew her to him. Her breath came more quickly at the proximity, her body scenting its mate.

"If you don't understand by now that I think you're the sexiest woman alive, I'll fuck you right here, right now to get my point across." His words were mild, but she felt a spark light in her belly at the threat. She wanted that. Fuck, yes, she did.

If he got inside her, she'd lose all perspective.

"I meant that you look pale. You've lost weight." She squawked with indignation when he ran his hands down her sides, brushing past her breasts to frame her waist. He scowled into her face. "And I could use those circles under your eyes as a landing pad for my spaceship. What the hell, Beth? Is this all because I told you I was falling in love with you?"

"No." Partly. His declaration had sent her into a blind panic. Not because she didn't want it, but because she did.

It made sense in her head, but she knew that as soon as she tried to explain, he'd refuse to accept it. And that didn't work for her.

"Then what gives?" Casting a sharp glance around the garage, she saw him take note of the pile of invoices, the parts stacked on the floor. The man wasn't an idiot, and she watched him connect the dots. "You're working yourself into the ground so that you can contribute to that balloon payment."

"We're all pulling double time to make that bill." Jerking out of the circle of his arms, she bent to pick up her coveralls. When she stood, she noted that he was staring at her ass. Normally noticing that would set her on fire.

Now? The set of his lips told her that he'd noticed that her little spandex shorts had gotten a little baggy.

"You're going to make yourself sick." He blanched as soon as he spoke, and she exhaled a breath of pure fire. He held up a hand to placate her, asking her to hold on.

"I didn't mean it like that." His eyes narrowed. "Whether you had to watch yourself or not, I'd be on your ass about this. You're working too hard. You're not sleeping, obviously not eating. That's enough to run anyone down."

She lifted her chin. No way was she going to admit that he was right. Rigidly, she pointed at the takeout bag. "You brought food, right? So let's eat. Then I can get back to work."

"I don't think so, babe." He moved so fast that she didn't see him coming. Like a linebacker, he tackled her, lifting her up and over his shoulder, hefting her like a sack of potatoes.

"Oh, I don't think so." Her words were full of venom. "Put me the fuck down, Ford. Now."

In response, he cupped her ass in both hands. She gasped as he made a thorough examination. "Needs to be fattened back up. Don't worry, I'd still hit it."

Outrage choked the words in her throat as he balanced her over his shoulder with one hand and snatched the takeout bag with the other. She slammed her fist against the broad muscles of his back as he carried her up the steps and through the door that led to the house.

Mamesie and Jo were in the kitchen when Ford came storming through with her over his shoulder. Mamesie's full lips parted with surprise, but Jo cocked her head, and Beth could see a smidgen of respect on her sister's face. She narrowed her eyes, but before she could yell at her sister, Ford had carried her to the stairs.

At the top, he paused, and she smirked. "I'm not telling you which one. Put me down."

She felt him shrug, which moved her body up and down. "Process of elimination, then."

Why was he being so stubborn?

"Nope." He opened and closed Jo's door, then Meg's. The third one he grunted, then hauled her in, shutting the door behind them. Bracing herself to be thrown on the bed, she was surprised when he instead slid her gently down in front of him, settling her on her bed softly.

Drawing her knees up to her chest, she hugged them tightly and looked up at him with curious eyes. "How did you know this one was mine?"

He snorted softly, settling himself beside her. He pointed at each object as he listed it. "Poster of dude playing the piano. Poster of chick playing the piano. Stack of those little booty shorts you love so much."

"I don't think I'm the only one who loves them." She sniffed, eyeing him from the corner of her eye. "And for your information, those posters are of Lang Lang and Martha Argerich. They're arguably the best contemporary pianists of our time."

She watched as he studied the posters, then turned back to her with a sly grin. "I still like Coldplay."

"Coldplay has its merits." When he undid the sack of takeout, she accepted the cardboard container that he handed her, even though the spicy scent made her stomach roll. "Chris Martin is no Lang Lang, but he's talented."

Ford handed her a plastic fork, nudging her container open. "Your music wasn't classical piano, though, right? Not the stuff you wrote."

"I thought you didn't listen to my music." She smirked. "Since it reminded you of what a bastard you'd been to me."

"That was then." He shrugged simply, opening a foil wrapper that contained his burrito. "I've checked out your YouTube channel."

"You what?" She sat up straighter. It was insane that those simple words made her feel so exposed, since the entire point of a YouTube channel was to get her content out there for others to find. Still, the thought of Ford listening to something that she'd birthed from within herself…

She wondered if he realized that the song she'd posted this week was about him.

"You have almost a million subscribers to your channel." Finished with his burrito, he removed a foil packet of tortilla chips and a plastic container of salsa. "Doesn't that help with your finances some? You make money off views, right?"

She appreciated that he hadn't tried to offer them money. She knew that what he had now was a drop in the bucket compared to his former fortune, but if he had enough that he was searching for a new investment, then he had at least six figures more in his bank account than she did in hers.

But he wasn't trying to give her charity. He wasn't trying to take things over. He was treating her like she was capable. And she appreciated it more than he could possibly know.

"Views are monetized, yes." She poked at her salad. He glowered until she scooped a bite into her mouth. "Thing is, I don't have the time to put up that much content. Just one song every month or two."

She chewed. She loved the taco salad from Mamacita's, but it tasted like dust in her mouth. She'd lost weight because she just hadn't been hungry much lately.

"And of those million subscribers, only a small fraction actually watch the new video when it's released." She shrugged. "It works for me, but no, it doesn't add much to the bank account."

He seemed to accept that, polishing off the chips and salsa while she struggled to eat half of her salad. When she'd eaten enough to suit him, he tugged the container from her hands, closed it and set it on her bedside table.

"Shirt off."

She felt her face form the lines of what her sisters called her *what the actual fuck* look.

He waited, and she shook her head.

"I have to get back to work. I don't have the time for this." She crossed her arms over her chest when he tugged at the hem of her tank. "Plus I can't say I'm in the mood after you told me I looked skinny and tired and hauled me through my own house."

"Beth." He fixed her with that intense stare of his, his expression serious. "Take off your shirt."

Damn it.

Part of the chemistry between them was rooted in the way they played with their power exchange. And even though she wasn't feeling particularly sexual at the moment, she found herself doing what he asked, tossing the tank top aside.

"Bra, too." Not waiting for her this time, he reached behind her back and unhooked the plain purple cotton garment. Sliding it down her arms, he pulled it off.

She expected him to cup her breasts, to toy with the piercing that he loved so much. She wasn't sure what to think when, instead of playing with her, he eased her back on her bed.

"Roll over onto your stomach." He patted her lightly on the ass. "Do you have any lotion? Oil?"

Huh?

"I have some sweet almond oil in my bedside drawer." She gestured lazily, but the prone position was somehow making her sleepy, despite the fact that she hadn't been sleeping well at all lately.

"Perfect." Retrieving the bottle, he squirted some into his hands, cupping it in his palms to warm it up. "I know you've been dying to try anal sex. No time like the present."

"Jackass." Still, she couldn't help the soft laugh, even as she tried to get her stomach to settle from the food she'd forced into it.

"Be nice, or I won't do this." Tipping his palm over above her back, he drizzled the warm oil down her spine. With a flat hand, he slicked it over her skin, then nudged her over so that he could climb onto the narrow bed and straddle her hips.

"Haven't had many boys in your room, huh?" She felt him shifting above her, trying to get comfortable. "How do you sleep on this thing?"

"Well, unlike you, I don't sleep crossways and spread-eagle." Pillowing her head on her hands, she moaned as traced a line beneath her shoulder blades with his thumbs. "And I've had plenty of boys up here. It works. You just have to get all nice and… tight."

"Temptress." Still, the hands stroking over her back continued what they were doing, the touches meant to soothe rather than arouse. He worked at a tight spot at the base of her neck, and she pushed into the good kind of hurt that his fingers found.

"Your hands are swollen." He worked his way down her arms, and she could hear the frown in his voice as he worked on her grease-smudged hands. "I told you you've been working too hard."

"They are?" She hadn't noticed, and an alarm bell started to ring in her head. His soothing touches quickly melted her concern.

"Yeah." Finished with her hands, he worked his way back up her arms. Sliding his hands into her hair, he started to rub the muscles of her scalp in a way that made her go cross-eyed with pleasure. When he stopped, she gurgled a protest. "Hey."

"You're warm, too. Way warmer than usual." He stopped rubbing her back, and she could all but hear his thoughts racing. "Are you sure you're feeling okay?"

"Yes." The response was automatic, but she found herself quickly scrolling through her mental checklist. Swollen hands, slightly feverish. Weight loss and fatigue, a stomach that struggled to digest what she'd put into it.

Damn it. How had she been so stupid?

She hadn't been feeling great for the last week, but she'd really thought she was just working hard and stressed about money. For all the attention that she paid to trying to keep herself healthy, she hadn't considered that what she'd been experiencing was a flare-up.

"What is it?" Ford rolled her over suddenly, and she struggled to smooth her features into blankness, even though her heart started to beat triple time.

She wasn't special. She was one of thousands of people who had lupus, a condition in which her body basically attacked itself.

But not all of those people had almost died from a sudden, wicked onslaught of symptoms. Not all of them had lost their careers and saddled the people they loved with such massive burdens that they feared they might never crawl out from beneath them.

This—this was why she couldn't let herself get too attached to Ford. She already fought not to buckle under the guilt every single day of her life. She couldn't add to it with another person that she was dragging down into the dirt.

More than that, what if she actually did die next time? It was too late for her not to love her family, and her family to love her in return.

But she didn't need to add anyone else to that list.

"I'm fine." Closing her eyes, she let Ford pull the covers up around her as she feigned sleepiness.

"Thank you for this. I just need some sleep—you were right."

"Good girl." The bed dipped beneath his weight, and an invisible fist squeezed her heart when he pressed a soft kiss to her forehead. "I'll talk to you later. Get some sleep."

With her eyes squeezed shut, she waited until she knew he'd gone, then sat straight up in her bed. Holding out an arm, she examined the pale skin.

Yup. There was the start of the nasty rash. She hadn't been paying attention. Her mouth was dry and her joints were stiff and sore, though she'd chalked that up to the physical labor she'd been doing.

How could she have been so *stupid*?

She needed to go to the ER to get checked out. The memory of the last time this had happened flashed in her mind's eye—the time her symptoms had come on so strong and fast, her body deteriorating so quickly that she almost died. Her pulse started to thunder, fear of a repeat making her nauseous.

But...a trip to the ER cost money. Money they didn't have, especially right now. She winced as she thought of the balloon payment—of how deeply they were all rooted in this home.

She hadn't had a flare-up since that first time because she took excellent care of herself. She ate well, exercised, took handfuls of prescribed vitamins and supplements. There was no way it could be as serious this time, and if she dragged her ass to the ER when it wasn't really necessary, she'd collapse beneath the weight of the guilt.

She'd be fine. She just needed some rest.

Arranging herself on her pillow, she ignored how painful it was to move her limbs. Gulped some water from the bottle on her nightstand to counteract the dry mouth.

If she'd been awake for it, she would have been surprised at how quickly the fatigue dragged her down into sleep.

"Baby girl, I thought you said you had an eight o'clock oil change this morning." Jo pushed into Beth's bedroom, the words piercing through her feverish dream. She jolted awake, staring wide-eyed at her sister as her brain struggled to work.

She couldn't move. Everything hurt. And something was wrong with her breathing. Her mouth opened, her chest moved, but she just couldn't get enough air.

She watched, paralyzed, as her sister's eyes widened in terror. Jo bolted across the room, gathering her in her arms, pressing on her back and chest as if trying to force the air into Beth's lungs. Beth felt her sister shake against her, or maybe it was her shaking. The voice that echoed around the room in a scream, though, that wasn't hers, because she couldn't draw in enough air to make a sound.

"Mamesie! Meg! Amy! Help!"

CHAPTER SEVENTEEN

THE NEXT MORNING, Ford drove the streets of Boston's South End, unable to settle. Something was up with Beth.

Something more than her being spooked at the fact that he'd told her he could fall in love with her.

He thought of the way she'd looked yesterday, the weight she'd lost apparent in her sunken cheeks. Her skin had been so pale that it was almost transparent.

She'd brushed aside his concerns about her temperature and swollen hands, telling him she hadn't been sleeping very well and was just tired.

His instincts said it was more than that. She'd shared that she'd been sick, sick enough that it had forced her to change her life.

But she still hadn't trusted him enough to tell him what, exactly, had happened. He'd wanted to wait for her to open up to him, to give her that respect.

Something wasn't right.

He ignored the blaring horns and screeching tires of the car between him as he swung the SUV to the side of the road. Lifting his hips, he worked his phone from his pocket. Pulling up his browser, he tapped out the words with his thumb.

beth marchande illness

The first few news articles that came up were fairly generic, with headlines like Local Girl Cancels Piano Tour Due to Health Reasons. While Beth had achieved something that very few people did—a recording contract—she still hadn't been that big a name. Piano enthusiasts knew of her, as did people who were into cutting-edge music, but she hadn't achieved the widespread popularity of the Gagas and Katys and Rihannas of the world.

His frustration grew as he scrolled through. Finally, on the tenth entry, he saw words that caught his eye—words she'd written, it looked like. An entry on the front page of her website, which was no longer actively updated.

Clicking on it, he was greeted with a breathtaking image. There was his girl, her sleek curves outlined in a fitted black sheath that formed a sexy V in the front. The sheer black sleeves of the jacket she wore over it muted the prismatic colors of her ink, but the bright hues still shone through.

She was seated on the bench of a piano—a fancy one to his eye, not that he really knew the difference—with her legs crossed demurely, one hand resting lightly on the keys. Her legs were bare, the tattoo work there peeking out teasingly from between the satin ribbons that wound from her high-heeled pumps to wrap temptingly over her calves.

Her hair had been tamed back into a sleek bun, but he smiled when he noted that it was cotton-candy pink. She smiled brightly out at the camera, a young woman with the world at the tips of her fingers, but he frowned, tracing his fingers over the image of her face.

Some makeup artist had worked their magic, smoothing out Beth's naturally rosy skin, doing that stripy thing Peyton used to do—was it called contouring?—and adding smoky stuff to her brilliant blue eyes to make them pop. Her lips were glossed a bright red, her eyebrows penciled in dramatically.

She looked gorgeous. Stunning.

But he liked her better in her coveralls with grease on her nose.

Scrolling down, he found the message on the homepage—a note from Beth to her fans.

I know many of you are disappointed that I've canceled the remainder of my tour. I'm very sorry to have to announce this, but due to an emergency with my health, I will not be rescheduling these dates or booking any other tours in the near future. I do not make this announcement easily, and I want to thank all of you for participating in this beautiful musical journey that I've been on for the last few years.

Bless,
Beth

The message was vague, just as she had been with him, but as he scrolled down to the comments he started to get more information. There were the inevitable nasty comments from the trolls. As he read some of the shit that people had thrown at her, his temper rose.

One long comment caught his eye, and as he read it, he found himself freezing.

PIANOGRRL94:

My sister is an ER doc in Cincinnati and I got the scoop. Beth was admitted in the morning before that first show she canceled and was moved to the intensive care unit. She was diagnosed with an autoimmune disorder called lupus.

KEYKEYSKEYS:

So? Lots of people have autoimmunes. My brother-in-law has Crohn's but he still gets his ass out of bed and goes to work every day. She's a lazy bitch

ADAM4732:

So is she going to reschedule her shows?

PIANOGRRL94:

You guys are assholes. She was admitted because her entire body shut down. I guess she'd been ignoring that she felt sick because she thought she just had concert fatigue. She almost died. Like, my sister didn't think she was going to make it. It's not advisable for her to tour anymore.

ADAM4732:

Why is your sister telling you this? Isn't there patient confidentiality shit that she's supposed to have?

PIANOGRRL94:

Whatever, guys. Just though you might want to know.

Beth had almost died.

Things began to click into place. The way she no longer drank, her inexplicable devotion to salads. The shroud of reserve that seemed to cover her at all times.

She was having a setback—he would have put every dollar that he had left in the bank on it. But why on earth wouldn't she just tell someone or go to the hospital? Why would she try to convince him that she was fine?

The balloon payment.

"Well, fuck." Beth was nothing if not stubborn, determined to prove that she was still capable of everything she'd been able to do before she got sick. She'd been so angry at her family for trying to cover for her, to make the payment without her, that she'd gone and made herself sick over it.

Anger and frustration radiated up his spine, exploding through his fingers as he pulled up his contacts and hit Beth's name. Putting it on speakerphone, he pulled away from the curb and started to drive, hanging a quick U-turn in the middle of the busy street, leaving honking and swearing behind him.

"What?" It wasn't Beth that answered, but one of her sisters.

"I think Beth's sick again," he blurted out. "I think she's hiding it because she'd worried about money."

"No shit, Sherlock." It was Jo, he was pretty sure. The acid in her tone was her signature, but it didn't melt away the worry that was there as well. "We're at Boston Medical Center. She didn't get up for her first appointment today, so I went into her room and she wasn't breathing."

"What?" Ice was a frigid spike that slammed into the length of his spine. "No. What's happening?"

"She's in the ER." Jo's voice was tight, and Ford

felt her pain as well as his own. "It's…they say it's not as bad as it could be. I don't know what she's told you—"

"She refused to tell me shit, so I just looked it up." He didn't even feel guilty. "I know what happened before. I know that she almost…died."

"Yeah." On the other end of the line, Jo's voice shook. "It's not that bad this time. We just can't believe she hid it from us. I can't believe I didn't see."

"She didn't want you to see." Ford sighed, taking one hand from the wheel to wipe the sweat on the thigh of his jeans. "Look, I'm on my way."

She thought that Jo might tell him not to come—not that he would listen—but instead she made a humming sound.

"Good."

"This is unacceptable, Elizabeth Serena Marchande."

"I'm sleeping." Beth squeezed her eyes shut. The touch of her mother's familiar hand on her brow had them flying open again.

The women of her family were gathered around her hospital bed in a tight ring. All of them were pale, clearly having lost sleep over the last twenty-four hours, and not a single one of them was smiling.

"Beth." Pulling up a hideous olive-green chair to the bed, Meg sank down into it, leaning forward to clasp her sister's hand. "What the hell were you thinking?"

She'd been thinking that she was avoiding placing a bigger financial burden on her family, and yet here they were. Another hospital bill and stress.

Sister of the year award did not go to her.

"Do you have any idea how scared I was when I went into your room yesterday morning?" Normally Jo would be the one right beside her, soothing her and offering comfort. Instead, her fiercest sister was standing at the end of the bed with her feet planted shoulder-width apart. Her arms were crossed over her chest, and her expression was terrifyingly blank. "I thought you were dying. *Dying*, Beth. Do you understand?"

"I—" She had no words. No excuse. She'd been trying to do the right thing, and yet she'd fucked it right up.

"Hi." Ford poked his head into the room. Her heart leaped at the sight of him, sinking again when she saw the ferocity on his face. She swallowed past a suddenly thick throat as her family greeted him, let him into the room, then filed out to give them some privacy. She was more than a little shocked by the courteous nod that he and Jo cast each other's way as they passed.

Great. She'd made a mess of her entire family, but her closest sister and her boyfriend had bonded over it. Fan-fucking-tastic.

Ford circled her bed, settling himself in the chair Meg had vacated. Beth studied him with trepidation.

Was he her boyfriend? If not, what was he? They hadn't been back together for very long, and yet she felt as though he carried a piece of her heart around in his pocket.

It was terrifying.

"Before you say anything, you should know that I went digging online. I know about your lupus." Beth winced. Ford shook his head. "I wish you'd shared that with me. Beth, you almost died."

"You think I don't know that?" Her voice was rough, groggy from all of the medications that were currently pumping through her system.

"Beth." He caught her hand. She tried to yank it back, but instead he laced their fingers together. "Talk to me."

She pressed her lips together. She hated this. Hated it all.

"Forget the guilt over the money part." She choked out the words. "This is how I feel. When you have a brush with death, and you survive, it's a new beginning. Treatment has been successful, so it's like… it's like people expect that that chapter of your life is over. They'll treat you with kid gloves, but the focus is on picking up and carrying on. Moving past it."

She swallowed, trying to find the right words.

"There can't be a return to normal because normal is gone. I'm not the same person I was before. I monitor myself constantly, and yet I'm in denial." She waved a hand around the room. "Like, hello. I've been waiting for the other shoe to drop, and I still missed it somehow."

"Oh, baby." He tried to tighten his hold, but she tugged her hand away. The simple touch was too much.

"Survival is a lonely place," she started, looking down at her own hands, which she twisted in the sheets. "But for me it's the way it has to be. You say you're falling in love with me, but how can you fall in love with all of this? I could get sick again, really sick, at any time. I got my life back, and I want to live it, but how can you treat me normally now? You'll be monitoring my every movement, since I've proven I can't take care of myself. That's no way to live."

"Do you think less of me for losing my money?" Sitting forward, he braced his hands on his knees, wraithlike eyes fixed on her figure.

"What?" She shook her head. "Of course not."

"You don't think I'm less capable because I did some really stupid things?" His voice was mild.

She got the point. Pinching her lips together, she studied his face. Her entire life, people had called her stubborn.

Turned out she had nothing on Ford Lassiter.

"Get some rest, baby girl." Extending one of his arms, he tugged her hand into his again, holding it tightly. "I'm not going to let go."

CHAPTER EIGHTEEN

"YOU HAVE AN appointment to change a transmission," Ford reminded Beth as he pressed a light kiss to her lips. She moaned and twined her arms around his neck, rocking her hips into his until he saw stars. "You're the one who wanted to go back to work already."

"I know, I know." Rising onto her toes, she slid her lips down the column of his throat. Growling, he pressed her back into his front door, covering her still too-thin frame with his body. "I had to run over and see you quickly between appointments, though. I'm missing you."

"Missing me or my cock?" Grinning, he turned her so that her breasts were pressed against the door. She was in her standard uniform of tank top and tight little shorts underneath coveralls that she'd tied around her waist.

They hadn't had sex in the full week since she'd been released from the hospital. First, it had been because the doctors hadn't allowed any strenuous exercise—she needed to rest.

Now it was because they hadn't had time. Beth had filled her schedule back up with appointments, desperate to make up the cash they needed for that big payment.

At least she was eating again, and sleeping because she'd been prescribed something for it. She was still too skinny, but she'd put on a couple of pounds, which was a relief to them all.

"How much more time do you have?" Growling with frustration, he clasped her waist, sliding his hands up to cup her breasts, toying with her piercing through her shirt the way he knew she liked. She pushed her ass back into his pelvis, rubbing it over his growing erection.

"Five minutes," she panted, placing her hands flat on the door. The sight of that, of her choice to assume a position she knew really did it for him, had his arousal cranking up to scorching levels.

Not enough time to get them both off. But at least he could send his girl off with a smile on her face.

"Keep your hands where they are." Leaving her bent over, he undid the knot she'd made at the waist of her coveralls. Letting them fall to the floor, he gathered the back of her little shorts in his fist, tugging until the elastic material slid between her cheeks.

"What will get you off right now?" Sliding his

other hand over her stomach, he grabbed the front of her shorts as well. Alternating where he pulled, he tugged the taut material back and forth through her dampening cleft, and her hips rocked with the rhythm.

"Just…treat me like I won't break." She dipped her head, her loose waves of hair falling into her face. "Whatever you want, just be rough."

The remaining blood from his brain drained south. He was hard as stone, and the need to sink inside that sinful cleft of hers was blinding.

No time. But he could make her feel good.

"Don't move." Letting go of her shorts, he left them as they were, where they'd ridden up and were wedged into the cleft of her ass. It left her round cheeks open to his view.

He hesitated for a moment. Those cheeks weren't quite as round as they usually were, and he reminded himself that she was still on the mend. If he was rough with her, would it hinder her healing?

"Come on already." She canted her ass back at him, impatience thick in her voice. "Three minutes. Should I do it myself?"

"You little brat." Growling, he lifted his hand and brought it down on her right cheek. She cried out, the sound swallowed by the audible smack of his palm on her ass.

"Is that what you wanted?" He delivered a second smack to her other side, then a series of lighter ones between her legs, right over her center. Her body tightened as he slid fingers between her legs, pushing beneath the stretched-out fabric of her shorts.

"You know it is." She clenched around him as he tucked his fingers inside her. Closing the space between them, he covered her body from behind with his own, using his free hand to work into her bra and pluck at her pierced nipple.

She was right. He'd developed a bit of a fetish about it. If he had his way, he'd convince her to do her other one, too.

"I wish I could be inside you right now." Knowing the words would bring her closer, he pistoned his fingers between her legs while roughly pinching the small gold hoop in her nipple with his fingers. "My cock is so hard it hurts, wanting to be inside you. This will just have to hold us both until we have time."

Scissoring the fingers inside her, he found the soft, fleshy spot that always made her scream. This time was no different, and when he rubbed the pad of a finger over it, she exploded around him, crying out and rubbing her breast into his palm hard, begging for him to tug on it.

When her shudders subsided, she kept her palms flat on the door, panting to try to catch her breath. Withdrawing his fingers, he hugged her from behind, pressing his lips to the back of her neck.

"I love you, Beth." His voice was rough, his body

tense as he waited for her reaction. Or for her to fucking thank him again, like on that episode of *Friends*, Ross with that girl he'd met in China. "You don't have to say it back. But I wanted you to know, I'm not falling anymore. I'm fully there."

Placing her hands over his, where they were clasped at his waist, she was silent for a moment—long enough that his nerves began to flock through his veins like migrating birds. Then she purred, a sound of pure satisfaction, tilting her head back to look him in the eyes.

"I love you, too." She swallowed, and he watched the line of her throat as she turned in his arms. "It scares the shit out of me, but you already knew that."

Rising to her tiptoes, she pressed a kiss to his lips. "And with that chitchat, I've got to go."

"One more thing." He ran his hands through his hair as she straightened her shorts, tugging her coveralls back up. "And hear me out."

Looking up from the knot she was tying, she arched an eyebrow.

"I know you're still stressed about money. And I know that there's a good chance you guys aren't going to make that payment." Her face fell, and he swore.

He hating seeing her unhappy. He wanted to do everything he could to keep her from being that way. Which, actually, was where this idea had sprung from.

"You'd better not be offering to pay it for us." The fire that sparkled in her eyes was blue flame. While she was in the hospital, he'd actually considered offering.

He didn't much like his chances among all five Marchande women on the warpath. They were proud; he understood that. He wouldn't insult them when he knew there was no way they'd say yes.

Which had birthed his idea.

"So first, let me remind you of some of my credentials." Straightening, he held up a hand to tick them off on his fingers. "I started Lassiter Hotels at the age of twenty-three. I used my own money because I wanted to be more than a trust-fund kid. I made my first million by age twenty-five and grew a single hotel into a global conglomerate."

"Uh-huh." Her voice was wry, but he saw the flicker of curiosity on her face. "Is this your idea of sexy talk?"

"Shush." She snorted, and he took it as a sign to continue. "I also went on to lose most of it, but I've been looking for a new opportunity. Not necessarily the one that would make me the most money, but one that felt right."

"Keep going."

"There are a lot of hotels in Boston. A lot of motels, a lot of B-and-Bs. But today people are so overly stimulated by devices and social media that they're wanting something simpler. A more authentic experience."

"You sound like a commercial." She rolled her eyes. "Get on with it."

"The very first time I visited your garage, I noticed that you have a large, rather oddly shaped lot. There's a lot of wasted space. Space that could be used." Normally in a sales pitch he pulled out all the stops, but right now he stopped. "Now, if you hate this idea, or your family hates it, that's fine. I'll think of something else. But I wanted to present this to you."

"Can't hate it if you don't get on with it." She tapped a finger on the door. "I have about thirty more seconds."

"Microhotels are the next big thing." He paused, searching for the right words. "What I'm proposing is that I lease a share of your land from you to build one of these. It will simply look like another house on the grounds but will be able to accommodate sixteen or so guests at a time. And I think you'd be solidly booked."

Beth furrowed her brow, trying to take it all in. "Who owns the structure then, if it's on our land? What happens if we hate it? Who runs it?"

"Those are all details to be discussed," he started, feeling the familiar thrill of a new project creeping into his veins. "But my suggestion is I—or rather, the company I will set up—will assume responsibility for building a plan that you approve of, on land that I lease a share of for a five-year term, to be re-negotiated at that time. At the end of that term, the deal can be renewed or canceled. If it's canceled, you would have the option to purchase the structure at wholesale, and I guarantee you, by that time you'll have made plenty to do so."

Beth's face was expressionless, but he knew she was turning it over in her head. He wasn't expecting her to tackle him into a hug, pressing her lips into his neck.

"I like it. I mean, I have to think about it. And tell the others and see what they think." Her eyes were bright, and he knew she was imagining the possibilities. "But if it will help us keep our house…wow."

Pulling back, she looked at him, and he was alarmed to see a sheen of tears in her eyes.

"Oh, God, don't cry." Alarm coursed through him. "I can't handle it if you cry."

"I'm not crying." With a giant sniff, she slid from his arms and opened the door. Looking back over her shoulder, she grinned. "You're kind of awesome, you know that?"

"I'll show you how awesome I am later." Propping open the screen door, he sank a hand into her hair and kissed her deeply, sweeping his tongue over hers. "I bought something I think you're going to like. Hint, it involves some clamps and your very pretty nipples."

"Fucking tease." She pushed through the door, then stopped short. "Um, hello."

"Well, hello there." A man in an impeccable suit stood at the top of the steps leading to Ford's house. An Armani suit, Ford recognized at first sight.

The man was almost as tall as Ford, and they shared the same lean build, the same thick golden hair, though his was sprinkled with salt and pepper. Looking past the man to the curb, Ford noted the sleek black town car that no doubt had a driver whose name the man didn't know, instructed to wait there for however long the man felt like leaving him there.

"Hello, Ford." The man smiled down at Ford, and Ford felt barriers that he'd only recently let down slamming back into place. "Aren't you going to introduce me to your lady friend?"

"This is Beth." He ran a hand down her back, a gesture of possession. Holding on to her, he smiled, but the movement felt stiff, frozen.

"Beth. This is my father."

"Aren't you going to invite me into your...home?" Bruce Lassiter rocked back on his heels, his expression as he looked at the house Ford had purchased showing exactly what he thought of it, which wasn't much. Beth had had to leave, and Ford was incredibly glad. "I had planned to drive the Beamer, but when I discovered which neighborhood you lived in,

I thought better of it. Imagine leaving that parked on one of these streets."

"Why are you here, Dad?" Crossing his arms over his chest, Ford shut the screen door behind him. There was no need to let his father inside—it would only invite more disapproval.

Bruce heaved a great sigh, as though Ford was a great trial to him. He probably was, but what Bruce didn't understand was that the feeling was mutual.

"My own son has been back in Boston for almost two months and hasn't come to see me." Bruce's words were an arrow, their aim true. "So I came all the way to the South End to see you. Try to talk some sense into you."

"We're not doing this again." Ford sighed, tilting his head up to the sky. Overcast and crammed with dense clouds, it was going to storm later. If the man upstairs favored him, the clouds would burst now and free him from this conversation.

"I just don't understand why you would live like this." Bruce cast his stare down the street, fixating on Ford's neighbor two houses down, who had a car on blocks parked in the middle of the lawn.

"Well, you've never understood me, so that's nothing new."

"Ford." Bruce fixed him with an exasperated stare. "I worked very hard to give you a life of leisure. You've never had to work, and I've never understood why you feel the need to drive yourself so hard. Let alone to live like…this."

Ford pinched the bridge of his nose.

"Especially now." Bruce was on a roll. "You have a trust fund waiting for you. What the hell are you doing in this shithole? Go back to LA and that woman you were engaged to. Or find a younger version. But I won't have a son of mine living like this."

"Dad, any success you've had is because it was handed down to you from Grandpa." A man not much better than Bruce, in Ford's opinion. "And I hate to break it to you, but I like it here."

And he really did. He never would have imagined it, but he was enjoying the physical labor of fixing up his own home. He liked looking at things after and knowing he'd put his own sweat into its creation.

"You've always been a little snot." Bruce smiled, but it was like ice. "So sure you were better than me."

"I've made it my life's mission to be better than you." The words were true, but they hurt Ford to say. He'd made his peace with the fact that he and his father would never see eye to eye, but he still had love for the man. Somewhere. You know, really deep down. "I wanted to work for a living. I wanted to prove that I could set a goal and turn it into reality. And heaven knows I wanted to treat women better than you ever have."

"That's why you bought clamps for your girlfriend's nipples?" Bruce laughed, tucking his hands into his pants pockets. "You can't fool me with this one, son. You're as kinky as your old man. Have been since you knew what sex was. Movies with some pain? Something rough? Yeah, you liked those. You think I didn't notice?"

Ford felt like he was fourteen again, watching one of those movies while his dad was nearby. It was nearly impossible to block the humiliation.

"And that girlfriend of yours? She looked like the type who likes it rough." Bruce smirked. "Don't tell me you don't give it to her good. The apple doesn't fall far from the tree."

"Get out." Nausea was bitter, coating Ford's throat. "I'm not going to stand on the steps of my own damn house that I bought with my own fucking money and listen to this shit. Don't come here ever again."

"Wouldn't dream of it." Holding out the paper bag he'd been clutching since his arrival, Bruce set something down on the step. "Brought you a little taste of the good life as a reminder. Wasted on you."

Ford pointed down the stairs. Bruce went, but Ford could hear his mocking laughter even after he'd gone.

CHAPTER NINETEEN

FINISHED WITH HER work for the day, Beth had come inside to grab a quick shower before she headed back to Ford's. Her body still tingled from his touch, and she felt a thrill of anticipation every time she wondered what he might have in store for her that night.

Her piano caught her eye as she walked through the house. She liked to play every day, but it had been over a week since she'd touched it.

Lifting the cover, she settled onto the bench. Stroking her fingers over the old keys, she paused for a moment then, grinning, started into a rendition of Coldplay's "Clocks."

She'd have to play it for Ford next time he came over. Which would probably be soon, if her family reacted to his idea the way she anticipated they would.

In her pocket she felt her cell phone buzz with an incoming call. She was tempted to let it go to voice mail, since she was just getting into the song, but if it was one of her family members checking on her, they'd freak out if she didn't answer.

"Hey, Ames." Her youngest sister's tattoo shop showed on the call display. As she'd guessed, one of her family members was checking up on her. "I finished work and I'm fine. Promise. Going to make some dinner, have a shower, head to Ford's."

"About that," Amy started. In the background Beth could hear the whine of the needles that Amy's other artists used. "Ford is here."

"What?" Beth frowned. "He doesn't strike me as the type to get ink."

"I had the same thought." Her sister's voice was not amused. "He's so drunk he might black out, though, so I'm assuming that has something to do with it."

"I just left his house two hours ago. He was fine," Beth protested, then thought of the sharklike man Ford had introduced her to. "Shit. His dad showed up just as I was leaving. It's got to have something to do with that. I'll come get him."

"Tank's already loading him into his van," Amy said. "He'll get him in the door, if you could just meet them there."

"On my way." Sliding her phone back into her pocket, Beth hesitated, then grabbed the keys to the sporty little Toyota sitting in her shop. She'd just serviced it, but her client, a friend from high school, wasn't picking it up until morning.

Beth didn't think Natalie would mind. It was an emergency. So she slid into the little red car, barely noticing the familiar smell of the cleaner she'd used to wipe down the dashboard—Natalie's daughter always had sticky fingers.

Ford wasn't the kind of guy to get sloppy drunk. He liked to be in control.

What the fuck had happened?

"He's in the tub." Beth had only met Tank, one of the artists who worked at Amy's shop, a handful of times. At six and a half feet tall and built like a linebacker, he lived up to his name. Beth didn't have to ask how he'd hauled a man who wasn't small himself all the way to the bathroom. "You'll want to help him shower. He reeks."

"Thanks, Tank." Beth shook his hand, giving it a squeeze. "Your next oil change is on me."

"I'll hold you to it." He jerked a thumb at his van, which was covered with spray-painted art. "The beast is making a clunking noise. I'll pop in next week."

Entering Ford's house, Beth closed and locked the door behind her. As she tossed her jacket on the bench where she always did, it occurred to her how comfortable she was here. Comfortable enough to let herself in and head to the en suite, which was where she assumed Tank had deposited Ford.

The medicinal aroma of scotch was strong enough

to make her feel drunk just from breathing the air. Gagging for a moment, Beth blinked down at where Ford was reclining, fully clothed, in the ancient avocado-green tub.

"This is not a good look for you." Dropping to her knees, she started to tug his T-shirt over his head. He grunted but let her undress him like a rag doll.

Unable to get him upright, she ran a hot bath for him. She ran soap over his body, into his hair, aware that his eyes were on her the entire time. He seemed slightly more sober when she tried to get him to stand up after, though he still wobbled when she toweled him off and dragged him to the bed.

"Let's sleep it off, Sir Lassiter." Arranging his naked frame on the sheets, she pulled the quilt over him, then stripped and climbed in on the other side. There wasn't a point in trying to get him to talk while he was still so drunk, so she'd wait until morning.

She was surprised when he rolled onto his side, facing her.

"My dad sucks," he slurred, reaching out to cup her cheek. He missed, stroking his hand over her nose and mouth instead. "All of him sucks. Not all of me sucks, but he reminded me of a part that sucks today."

"Figured there was a reason for the scotch spree." She pursed her lips. "Why scotch, dude? You're going to feel like shit in the morning."

"My dad knows I'm kinky." Ford frowned, trying

to focus. "Picked up on it when I was a teenager. He likes it. He's proud of it. Said the apple doesn't fall far from the tree."

Beth's stomach rolled.

"I shouldn't treat you like that." She watched him swallow—he needed some water. "Shouldn't be that kind of man."

Temper licked along her skin—not at Ford, but at the asshole who had spawned him. Ford was still settling into being comfortable with who he was. This was the last thing he needed.

She opened her mouth to argue, but Ford's eyes were already closed. He'd rolled onto his back. She thought he was already asleep, but he said one thing before he started to snore. One little thing, but it made her blood chill.

"I'm not good enough for you."

Ford smelled coffee before he even opened his eyes.

He needed some. Preferably a bucketful to soak his head in.

He pushed himself to a sitting position, yelping when the white light of morning blinded him. Stabbing pains pierced his skull, and he clutched his head in his hands, willing the pounding drums to stop.

There was a glass of orange juice and two tablets of aspirin on his bedside table. Beth. The woman was a fucking goddess.

Staggering into the bathroom, Ford brushed the

fuzzy feeling from his teeth, then showered away the alcoholic sweat. Pulling on the first shirt and track pants he found, he stumbled into the kitchen.

Beth was sitting at his table, playing with her phone while she sipped tea from a mug. His mug, one that said Lassiter Hotels.

He needed to get rid of that.

She watched as he seated himself beside her. Assuming the piece of dry toast was for him, he choked it down silently, aware that she had her eyes on him the entire time.

"Better?" she asked when he pushed the plate away. Cautiously, he took stock, then nodded. He wasn't great, but he'd do.

It wasn't until he chugged his own mug of coffee that his vision cleared enough for him to really look at Beth. She was there, which was definitely something, but her manner was…off. Stiff.

What the fuck had he done?

"Do you remember last night?"

He winced, rubbing his hand over the top of his head. "Yeah. It's hazy, but yeah. Right up until you hauled my ass into bed."

"Mmm-hmm." She set her mug down with a sharp click. "Do you remember what you said to me?"

"Ah…no." *Fuck.*

"I see." Nodding, she folded her hands together, then seemed to change her mind, holding one hand up as she ticked items off a list. "You told me your dad was an asshole. Granted, I only met him for a moment, but the way he stared at my tits made me inclined to agree."

Ford's stomach sank.

"Since we're not the sum total of our parents, that didn't bother me very much. What *did* get under my skin was when you compared yourself to him. Specifically, when you told me that you weren't worthy of me because you were a bad, bad man for being kinky like dear old dad."

"I—" The words brought it back. The humiliation that had come rushing in when his dad had mocked him for thinking that he'd distanced himself.

The sinking sensation that Bruce was right—that even after all the effort he'd put into it, he was cut from the same cloth.

"He's not wrong." Whether it was the shitty way he felt, the way the sun was still streaming into his eyes and blinding him, or the fact that he was just emotionally bankrupt after the night before—he said it, and he didn't even feel like taking it back. "Jesus, Beth. You, of all people, I shouldn't be fucked-up and rough with."

"Are you fucking kidding me?" She slammed her hands on the table, sending the coffee mugs flying. "Me, of all people? What the fuck does that mean?"

"You know what it means." He couldn't stop the words from flying out of his mouth, maybe because they needed to be said, his deepest fears seeing the light of day. "It means that I don't want to be responsible for sending you to the hospital again because I'm a perverted fucker!"

"I suppose it's missed your attention entirely that I like the fact that you're a perverted fucker." When he didn't answer, Beth stood, shaking her head. "I'm out of here."

He wanted to go after her, wanted to hold her down and claim her with his body until neither of them had any doubt about what they both really wanted.

So close on the heels of the shit with his dad, the thought both aroused him and made his stomach turn. He let Beth make her way to the front door, misery seeping from every pore.

Before she left, she turned around, glaring at him with those fierce blue eyes. She pointed with her index finger, and he couldn't look away. "I have a disease that affects my life. Yup, I do. You have daddy issues. We're both kinky as fuck, and we both need to get the hell over it. When you sort that shit out, you know where to find me."

Fuck, fuck, fuck.

CHAPTER TWENTY

HER SISTERS WERE being twitchy. All of them.

The three women were lounging around the garage as Beth checked the brake pads of an old beater some high school student had dragged in. He wanted the thing to run for a big date but couldn't afford the service. She'd traded him for some work around the garage and was pleased with the way her space sparkled.

An engine sounded outside, and her sisters all tensed. Beth looked around, wondering what she was missing that they were obviously clued in to.

The engine noise drew closer, and suddenly her sisters were on her. Meg ran a brush through the length of her ponytail, Amy scrubbed grease from her nose with a clean rag and Jo unzipped her coveralls so that they fell to the ground and Beth was obliged to step out of them, leaving her in a shirt and her shorts.

"What the hell, guys?" She tried to jerk away, but they clung to her like pandas to bamboo. Finally satisfied, they pulled away, letting her turn to greet the newcomer.

A shiny silver Porsche Turbo sat in the garage. It had a gigantic purple bow on it, and Beth's pulse went from zero to sixty as Ford swung himself out from behind the wheel.

She hadn't seen him, heard from him, even heard *about* him since she'd left his pathetic, hungover self sitting at his breakfast table. When she left she'd felt confident that he would get his shit together, but just this morning a tendril of worry had snaked its way into her gut, making her wonder if maybe he hadn't been able to overcome his mixed feelings about who he was and what he wanted.

"Got to get to work!" Amy held a condom in front of Beth's face, then tucked it into the waist of her shorts before scampering up the steps to the house. Meg followed her, laughing. Jo moved more slowly, and when she reached the top of the stairs Beth was amused to see her point to her eyes, then to Ford's again, mimicking the gesture she'd given him the first time he'd been over since he'd been back.

The garage was quiet with the chatter of her sisters suddenly gone—almost too quiet. Beth could hear the sudden thundering of her heart as she turned to face the man she loved, hoping, praying that things were going to be okay.

He stared right back. Finally, she cleared her throat and pointed at the Turbo. "What's with the bow?"

"You know how much I love this car," Ford started, closing the distance between them. He stopped with a thin ribbon of space still between them, and Beth yearned to press her body against him, to take in his heat. To take in *him*.

"I might have an inkling." For something to do, she ran a hand over the sleek silver hood.

"I love you more." Startled, she turned her gaze back to him. His expression was dead serious, his hands held out for her. Slowly, cautiously, she took them, a shudder of relief working through her at the feel of his skin on hers.

Looking from him to the car, she understood. "You are not giving me a Porsche. *Your* Porsche. No way."

"I needed something to demonstrate how I feel. How stupid I've been." He grinned crookedly, one side of his mouth curling up higher than the other. "It's this or a ring, baby. I figured you'd choose the car."

"Holy shit." She knew she was gaping; she couldn't help it. "You're insane. And playing dirty."

"I sure am. I'm a little messed up," he admitted, pulling her against him. Burying his face in her hair, he inhaled deeply, and she melted against him. "Look, I'm not miraculously all better. I have issues. You do too, you know."

She sniffed but said nothing.

"But I know one thing with absolute certainty. I want you in my life." Grasping her chin, he tilted her face so she looked at him. "Do you feel the same way?"

She wanted to make him work for it after what he'd put her through, but she didn't have the heart. Swallowing past a sudden burning lump of tears, she nodded, unable to speak.

He grabbed the end of her ponytail, wrapping it around his hand. She gasped when he tugged her head back, his smile turning from relieved to wicked. "Besides, when you finally agree to that ring, the Turbo will at least be in the same house again."

"You're so bad." She gasped when he tugged again, dipping his head to sink his teeth into the cord of her neck. She hissed out a breath when his free hand cupped her breast firmly, pushing her back until her ass hit the front hood of the Turbo. Wet heat rushed between her legs as he eased her back onto the hood, the way he had so many years before.

"Like it or not, it seems that I am," he agreed, sliding his hand down between her legs. She cried out when he rubbed his fingers over her clit, through her shorts.

"And I'm going to spend the rest of my life proving to you just how bad I can be. 'Cause that's what we both want."

* * * * *